Cara,

HAPPY BIRTHDAY '88

love

John

THE DUCHESS'S DIARY

THE DUCHESS'S DIARY

Robin Chapman

faber and faber

LONDON · BOSTON

First published in 1980
by Boudicca Books
Reissued, with revisions, in 1985
by Faber and Faber Limited
3 Queen Square London WC1N 3AU

Printed in Great Britain by
Whitstable Litho Ltd, Whitstable

© Robin Chapman, 1980, 1985

British Library Cataloguing in Publication Data

Chapman, Robin
   The duchess's diary
   I. Title
   823'.914[F]   PR6053.H363
   ISBN 0-571-13441-6
   ISBN 0-571-13442-4 Pbk

For Boo

PREFACE

This book is written in the form of a diary translated from an original manuscript. I have called it The Duchess's Diary *but, of course, the original would have had no title. It records the memories and actions, during the early months of 1616, of a young woman who had unwittingly become the model for a person known only in her fictional form: the Duchess who plays such an important role in the second book of* Don Quixote. *In her account María Isabel and her husband Jerónimo, the Duke of Caparroso, entertained Cervantes during the summer of 1608 when he was already famous as the author of the first book of* Don Quixote.

The diary makes no particular demands upon the reader's knowledge of Cervantes's masterpiece beyond what is universally known: that imagination is as unreasonable as reality. María Isabel's story is brief and complete. She believed herself to have been recognisably misrepresented in fiction. Then as now authors are not to be entirely trusted; our simplicities become their complexities.

The Diary

— another Wednesday and I can't talk any more to anyone.
I did try talking to the new chaplain but his shadow
reminded me of a giant peg doll and there is no way
of keeping warm in this stone box I now inhabit even
though the sun has shone every day since Epiphany but
has no power to melt the snow on the ash-heap mountains.
My husband knows how I loathe it here — his favourite
place, his weekly keep-up-appearances letter invariably says —
but in fact he never does come up here in winter because
by November he's killed all the game so their remains
may defile my beautiful house twenty miles away in the
valley, every corridor, hall, staircase which I used to love
a sawdust-stuffed mausoleum with glass eyes, tusked
snouts, brittle moulting wingspans strung on string.
Jerónimo lives for hunting. I used to go with him or he
sulked, big baby, a hawk fidgeting on my aching wrist
which was how our guest first saw me by the river where
the silver poplars grow so straight. Our guest, a medium
plump man with a long soft nose. Our guest. My famous
author.

It's half an hour later and I've prayed and I've decided
to decide that I've got to be calm as though none of this
had really happened to me but to someone else. I must
record it accurately with correct punctuation because I
may be deceiving myself as my husband in name said
over and over again when he had me carted up here,
bound with linen strips to my prayer stool, after our
Twelfth-Night dinner.

That dinner when I showed the whole world, well,
our twenty or so honoured guests, that is our utterly
local gentry with their greasy moustaches and blood-
pudding wives, my secret condition as it is known, the

always ready wounds out of which the doctor, Dr Villanueva, draws my bad humours as he calls them which cause my melancholy as he terms it. Every week. He was very fashionable when he first prescribed the treatment. The sutures on the inside of my thighs are what I mean, those never properly healed wounds which have had one benefit only during all these years: they've enabled me to refuse my bed to my husband because I simply cannot bear his weight and pressure on me. Jerónimo is sixteen stone at thirty-eight which is surely grotesque? But they shouldn't have talked about that book. That's why I lifted my skirts over the venison with juniper berries, because before dinner and during dinner that's all the conversation had been, was. They went on and on about it which shows that Jerónimo's deceiving himself when he says hardly anyone's read it, everybody had read it, then. Isn't it funny? they said, I've never laughed so much, they said, even the King's read it, they said. Didn't you entertain the distinguished author a few years ago? they said, smelling blood at a distance. Don't I remember some marvellous, expensive pantomimes with fireworks? they said, circling closer. And didn't your Italian steward play the part of the mad knight? Yes, but my husband dismissed him later, I said, he didn't run the house properly, he was too in love with amateur theatricals, he began to select our staff for their acting abilities. I was talking too fast, trying to laugh, trying to turn the conversation away. It came to a point, I said, when there wasn't a groom who wasn't declaiming speeches in the stables or a housemaid who wasn't dimpling and curtsying to herself as she emptied the chamberpots. We laughed but they wouldn't leave the subject alone, oh, no, they darted in for the kill. But don't you think it quite charming how he makes the squire take to the duchess, he's forever confiding in her, talking to her in her room? I screamed, not very loudly but some heads turned, I screamed, you don't understand, the author divided himself in two but cut me into little bits, we must distinguish between truth and fiction, I've told Jerónimo a hundred times we should sue for libel but he just laughs and says it's all harmless, a gentle joke, he doesn't see me chopped up in pieces and exposed as mad quite mad. All heads turned then and there was a hellish silence all round me and I was in a whirlpool, all the floating remnants of me being sucked in and down, down, but my husband came to the rescue, not my rescue you understand but the occasion's rescue, socially Jerónimo is very sensitive, we can all go in to dinner now, he said loudly, all this literary chit-chat has given me an appetite. He's full of such hearty incongruities which he binds together with a laugh like a whipped egg.

I didn't say a word throughout the first course or the second but their hostess's silence made no difference, nothing can stop people talking about this hideous book, about how widely it sells, about how many languages it's already been translated into, I'm a laughing stock in French, German, Italian, English, Chinese even, if the author's dedication is to be believed though he may be joking you never know with him he uses irony like a gelder's knife. My only consolation, and it's none at all really, is that he has made no profit from it. I hear he had to sell the copyright to the printers in order to finance the writing of the last chapters; he was hopeless with money, he said, good, I hope he dies in poverty as I'm sure I shall now.

The man sitting next to me at dinner, Count Braja, an elegant, epicene bachelor who sodomises shepherd boys and writes succulent pastoral verses elevating his pederasty, turned to me eventually and said, his rosebud lips glazed with butter (we cook with butter in Aragón not oil as is commonly supposed), he said, I don't think the book is unfair to you or your husband really. Glutinous smile. I read it with great attention remembering how hospitable you had been to the ageing author and knowing also what vultures such professional persons invariably are.

11

Winsome laugh. But in this instance I find he's been most circumspectly vague, don't you agree? He doesn't even name you with a name that is a teasing echo of your own, he employs no such vulgar device, he simply refers to Jerónimo and you, my dear María Isabel (Braja dared to use my christian names for the first time, I'm common property now, the book has given everybody licence to consume me) as the Duke and the Duchess. The fact is you could be anyone, he continued, mouth full, and even we who know you both, such a handsome couple, can find in his text no descriptions of your physical attributes, no parodies of your manners nor idiosyncrasies of speech, your husband's distinctive laugh, for example, is never heard, everything is quite blank, we read of a Duke and a Duchess, titles only, so the reader is left, and in my view this is the author's distinctive discretion, I do not think we need any longer doubt his genius, the reader is left to supply what characters he wishes to these two resonant shell-like forms, don't you agree? Simper. Still I kept silence, wrapping it round me, tighter, tighter. He said, had he referred to your husband's magnificent physique or to your exquisite form, I well remember your performance as the Princess Dulcinea and can readily believe you were for him the perfect embodiment of that unearthly beauty, what honours you bestowed upon him, had he gloried in celebrating you, in delineating for his readers' delectation your red-gold hair, emerald eyes, pearl-white cheeks, swan-like neck and those other hidden wonders of your youth and sex which were I not a sodomite I should pant and plague you to reveal to me so I might immortalise them in verse, had he done this, my dear delicious María Isabel, then indeed one might fault him for an understandable yet forgivable indiscretion. His voice had sunk to a lip-licked whisper, his face was too close to mine, the little air that was left between us was damp with sibilant aestheticism.

That's when I jumped on the table. Flung back my chair

and jumped on the table. Me. Yes! That's when I heard myself shouting look, look, you shall see! Was aware of my hands like rats scrabbling at the stiff brocade of my skirts, the silk of my petticoats, lifting them higher, bunching them around my waist screaming look, look, look at what this modest, discreet author who so amuses the whole world, look at what of all things he did choose to depict, did particularise, did delineate, did mention, speak of, write about quite unnecessarily so that you should all know without doubt that his supposedly anonymous Duchess was really me, me, me! These details, these unmentionable things, these open secrets which you've all whispered about, conjectured about for years, the Duchess María Isabel Echauri y Pradillo de Caparroso's indelible marks of chronic bad blood, she only appears sane in public, can only be kept quiet in private because she's drained continually of the melancholy, spleen, black bile poison of her innermost self, self, self, so septic her husband has to laugh her off all the time as if she wasn't there, poor man under that bluffness he's a tender soul in torment, she can't bear his touch, his weight, no wonder no presentable woman is safe from him, a meaty red-blooded man with normal appetites tied to a demented wife who looks like an angel spun from gold and glass but is a viper, toad—I didn't finish my hysterical protest because I slipped on the polished oak, falling backwards, my ugly sutures, sex, I'm very pretty just there, naked legs flailing at candles spilling wax, gold plates spewing food, crystal glass exploding, knives slithering, forks from Paris cavorting, these a new fad of my husband who now dragged me from the table as I kicked and screamed, let them look, let them look, hauling me bodily out of the chair-capsizing swell of our guests' disgust, shock, consternation, laughter escaping out of crackling whalebone, side-mouthed upheaval, she's unwell, it's the strain, you mean her lack of breeding, wait till I tell the Duke of Lerma, Guzmán, Her Majesty, they'll die of laughing, the Christmas season's

13

too much responsibility for someone like her, I said she looked peaky, too talkative, too bright-eyed, by which time I was strapped to this prayer stool in my bedroom with my turkey-cock husband gagging me with a silk scarf and shouting in my face, you stay quiet do you hear me? Pray! God help you, pray!

Thursday 27th January

I have been counting the days since the shortest day and I now know, I think, my arithmetic has always been more figurative than numerical, that today is thirty-seven minutes longer than that other day when the book, that book, was first placed so tenderly in my lap. In my house in the valley.

Jerónimo had come back from Zaragoza, breathless, frost-rimed, boyishly proud of the time he'd made on his new chestnut gelding, a big-boned, ugly thing with legs like ship's gun barrels, but even prouder of something else he'd achieved, the rumours were right, he shouted, banging into my room without a knock, still in his boots with the spurs clotted, it's printed at last, published at last after all these years, and everyone's saying it's better than the first, the sequel's better than the first book, Maribel! It's a triumph, masterpiece, feast of laughter, crazy cart-wheeling comedy, biting satire, razor-keen anatomy of society's ills but heart-warming, too, Maribel, eye-misting, wholesome, it's approved by the censors, both church and state, so a child can read it without harm, a priest without qualms, a lady without alarm.

Obviously Jerónimo had heard or read the recommendations of the printers whose professional enthusiasms are so much more reassuring to the public than the amateur assessments of critics who have nothing to lose from their opinions. Jerónimo smiled like an overweight lardy baby and I almost kissed him, except he was sweating, so pleased he looked to have pleased me at last, so happy

14

to have brought me what he knew would delight me more than anything else in the world, what I'd longed for, prayed for, given up hope of. I unwrapped it, a thick quarto volume, from its waxed paper. It was heavy in my lap, smelling deliciously of fresh print on good paper, uncut. I thought, I'll let it lie in my lap until my hands and legs stop trembling. Meanwhile I thanked my husband and he left me saying he hoped it would make me better and I said, I know it will, I know it will, and I was laughing as he shut the door, quite quietly for him, and I heard him crash down the corridor shouting for his valet to come and remove his boots. Peace, silence, the weight of that book.

I had hoped to find that the author had dedicated his work to me or at least to us, his hosts. It was a half-hope, no more. It was just possible he might have felt sufficiently grateful. After all, hadn't he said to me, yes, he had, at that private leave-taking he'd requested so charmingly, I don't deceive myself, he did say, I remember it exactly, he said, my dear Maribel, I'd allowed him in impulsive fondness the use of my childhood name (until that time the prerogative only of my husband and my personal maid, Juana), he said, because of you I have spent three months in heaven beside the Ebro. And I said, you must mean in spite of me? But he denied that very gently, saying, no, no, in this green and shaded place I have written more and better than ever before in my life, in fact I wonder if I shall ever be able to write so well again. You have been my inspiration, Maribel, you. But I saw at once, after the title page, that he'd dedicated the second part of his poetic history, as he called it, to the Count of Lemos, his latest patron presumably, whose hospitality had been more recently enjoyed, I suppose. Practical monster. My hand is shaking again, I must hold it still.

I was very strict with myself. I did not allow my eye to take in a word until I'd cut every page with a little gold knife my father gave me. It was very small and he'd

15

said it had once been used in sacrificial ceremonies in Mexico. I cut every single page, all five hundred and eighty-two of them, it took me more than three hours, a tantalising space in which I found myself panting with the effort as if I were running blindfold such was the self-control needed not to notice that in the middle of the book there were continual references to a Duke and a Duchess. And even when at last all those pages were cut I made myself, yes, forced myself to begin at the beginning so I should be able to judge his work as a whole, as an entirety in its own right, with a beingness, livingness belonging to itself, with its own internal laws and necessities, no matter what the inspiration had been (he'd talked to me so much about the proprieties of fiction, they were his passion and I'd thought I'd understood him), no matter how personally involved I might feel in the production of this already proclaimed masterpiece, this second and final part of the true history of Don Quixote.

And I was rewarded. What pleasure I took in the beginning. How I laughed. I read those opening chapters with as much pleasure, no, more, as I had read the closing chapters of his first book, that ever-widening river of invention which begins as a single spring, a lonely, tentative trickle meandering forward then back so that it almost loses itself in bone-dry midsummer but just as you think it's evaporated it meets another, heartier source from the same place and together the two rivulets bubble out again, become an absurd, argumentative confluence running ever more strongly until it comes to a small cliff's edge, the boundary of that local world, and tumbles over, and the author stops, steps back and sees his invention, I think, for the first time, sees it as a modest but glorious waterfall shot through with never-ending possibilities like interwoven rainbows. I know that's a fanciful description which probably describes not so much the first part of the first book as my enthusiasm for it, my fatal enthusiasm which led me to persuade Jerónimo

16

to honour the famous author's visit with masques and pantomimes portraying *our* imagined further adventures of *his* lunatic knight and squire.[1] To be fair Jerónimo hadn't needed much persuasion, he'd liked the book, too; even Jerónimo whose chief reading is usually game logbooks, his own and other people's. He often dismisses other people's as fantasy, snort, snort.

Juana came in a minute ago to clean this room but I've sent her away. She said, you sent me away yesterday, Miss Maribel, and the day before. She has always called me Miss Maribel, has always ignored my ennobled married state. I said, this room doesn't have to be clean, I don't want it to be clean, I want it to fill with dust and dirt, go away! Poor Juana, she's been faithful to me ever since she came from Galicia when she and I were girls. But she didn't grow and her eyes squint fiercely. She's a dumpy thing, a loving dwarf. She has plonked the broom by the door in protest. I can see it now if I turn round. I wish I were a witch, I could fly away on it. I think sometimes I'm more childish now than I was as a child because when I was seven I had proof that witches cannot fly. I saw one whom everybody expected to fly away but the woman had been bound so tightly she couldn't. She just sat in the cart taking her to the fire with a penitent's hood over her face. What did she do? I asked my father. She sold ointments and robbed the dead of their teeth, he told me. So I knew *then,* quite clearly. But now? I must return to my other room, get there somehow, I'll shut my eyes for a moment, cover them with my hand, feel the pulse in my forehead, is it too quick? Yes. Why? So quick. What has it remembered that I haven't? Oh, no! Yes, yes, it's Thursday. Oh, no. Yes.

[1] *Don Quixote, Part I*, was published in early January 1605. *Part II* in November 1615.

17

Friday 28th January

The doctor came, of course. Very soon after I remembered what day it was. Afterwards I insisted that he leave some brandy for me. I drank it all and slept away the rest of the afternoon and most of the night. Juana sat with me. Oh, if only I could understand exactly how much I persecute myself and how much others persecute me.

I was trying to remember how pleased I was when I began to read that book. My author writes just as he talks. It was his voice I heard as I read, not my own. What a joy it was to escape again with his heroes from their village in La Mancha, that village he so carefully chooses not to name. With what anticipation I went with them to the next village which he *does* name and which *does* exist, is there still, I imagine, El Toboso, family seat of the Princess Dulcinea, that unequalled beauty whom the squire describes as looking just like me but who exists only as a lie, a deception, not in reality at all, like me now in this hunting box among these hills. But I mustn't think about now, no, I will and must ignore now because I need to remember then, then when the book had first arrived and I hadn't yet reached the moment when he produces, bland conjuror, me, oh, yes, me. Well, Jerónimo too. But no one would recognise Jerónimo.

How I wondered how the squire would get round his huge lie left over from the previous book that he had already seen Dulcinea. What would he do now his master insisted he lead him to her palace in a real ramshackle village where the most imposing building was the parish church doubtless with a brood of storks learning to fly from the dilapidated belfry? I need not have wondered. He simply persuaded his master to let him go into the village alone, except he didn't even bother to do that, he just pretended and on his fake return passed off the middle one of three peasant girls who happened to be riding by on donkeys as me. My author has that kind of answer for everything. So there are *two* of me in the book, myself as the Duchess and another me as the figment of ideal beauty created by a lying peasant in the imagination of a deluded country gentleman. Did he think I'd be flattered? I'm jumping ahead again, I mustn't. I noticed too, it was like a shiver down the spine, that the Knight of the Sorrowful Countenance had become wiser, or should I say maturer, in his madness? And even more like his author, my author, but then so was the squire, as I said before he split himself most conveniently into two so he could talk to himself without fear of interruption. A happy division, a marriage of air and earth. And the squire half was much more conceited now, much more confident of his own cunning. Like the writer. Rather more slowly I began to be aware as that short day darkened so soon and I refused dinner and ordered more candles to be lit that the author had taught himself to write something quite unlike anything I had ever read before. Of course, I realise now I'd had the benefit of his instruction throughout that summer when he'd talked and talked, telling me how difficult it was to write a history which could be believed as real and enjoyed like poetry at the same time; how the events had to be plausible, the characters recognisable, the landscape solid and the whole of an intangible, never-seen-before beauty which the reader's mind and heart would know to be true: *this* is the world, how was it I had never noticed before? I paraphrase him badly but then he talked so much. And how effortlessly the river of his story flowed along, sunbright one moment, dappled by glancing shadows the next, then gloomed by a green tunnel! Its surface was always serene (not like this diary which bumps and jolts) but under it I sensed hidden snags, sudden declivities, weed-shrouded depths. I began without knowing why to hold my thumbs. I don't mean at the growing sense I had that he was bound to portray me, though I suppose that was part of it, no, I began to fear

19

for him, I mean his two heroes. By the time the knight had won himself a new title, that of Knight of the Lions, having dared to personal combat a circus lion who farted in his face, I decided to stop reading in order to discover what it was that gave this second book its unnerving quality. I decided, and I may be wrong, it may only be a part not the whole, that underneath that easy story lurks a machine which he builds in the first book and refines in the second. It works like this: the author pretends he's presenting a history written originally by an Arab and that he found the manuscript by luck on a bookstall in Toledo. He pays a student to translate it from Arabic into Castilian and then presents this translation to us with comments and jokes. So nothing appears as his own invention except his observations by the way. It is as if our existences are recorded in a language we don't understand. But they can be translated, oh, yes! Whole lives can be translated, very neatly, very easily, but they still won't make sense to *us* unless they're interpreted by a superior someone who understands everything, a sort of smiling doctor of the mind, our author, this author, my author who has broken me in pieces and scattered me like bread on the translucent surface of his endless prose. Oh, God, a piece of me has just been swallowed by a pike, another by a duck, I'll be gone soon.

Another pleasure, there were so many before I met myself hawking by the river—how fair I'm trying to be!— was the knowledge both knight and squire had of their earlier exploits being published. They know they are famous even before they set out again on these further adventures. It's no matter that their fame is ridiculous, fame is fame which like money confers dignity however disreputably it has been got, my father told me that, provided enough has been got, of course. So now people laugh at them behind their backs but to their faces are as courteous as their author was to me, so deferential to Jerónimo, so understanding with me. He had the knack of looking at you as if you were the most interesting person in the world. Why, oh why did I confide in him? I can't write any more today, words aren't my *métier*, they're his, his, his!

Saturday 29th January

A sparrow has just flown in at my window. I'd opened it for a moment, the effort was enormous, the latch is stiff and rusty, to see if I could smell any kind of spring. I've tried to shoo it out but it's whirred in panic behind the tapestry of Europa surprised by Jupiter, a frightened little brown-grey creature lost behind the larger-than-life convulsions of a bouncy, dimple-bottomed Flemish girl about to be mounted by a bull, Jerónimo had it hung here years ago, it reminds him of his bachelor days when he served in the Low Countries, though he wasn't really a bachelor, we'd been betrothed, but nothing more. It's a garish, vulgar fantasy. Scuttle, scuttle. Poor little bird, it's made me remember the old song about a lark which sang outside the prisoner's window until one day a hunter shot it. It's gone silent now. I must shut the window again, it's so cold.

I'm going to write out the text of my husband in name only's letter for this week. He always writes on Friday. I always receive it on Saturday. The chaplain has just brought it. Thank God, it's a murky yellow morning threatening snow and he cast no shadow. I'm copying it out so posterity may perhaps know how I am treated here. Madam, it reads, your chaplain and spiritual adviser together with Dr Villanueva inform me that you make haste to recover your wits at the pace of a tortoise. (He always writes in this constipated way.) Indeed your chaplain in particular can discern in you little but resentful apathy which scarcely conceals the lack of a contrite heart, a growing habit of unwholesome secrecy, a refusal to pray with him or submit to any spiritual guidance whatsoever

21

and a curious passion for lettuce. (That's true! I do long for lettuce! Perhaps it was this snippet of spy's information which prompted Jerónimo's tired simile of the tortoise?) A vegetable which you well know is hardly obtainable at this season yet you plague him with unreasonable requests for it. I must ask you to remember that I did not appoint this learned and reverend person to be your greengrocer but your intercessor with the Most High since only He can restore your mind to its former wholeness yet even He requires your compliance in this necessary undertaking. (I bet he sucked his thumb there, the handwriting of the next sentence looks slightly different.) I must also remind your ladyship that you have brought this isolation from the world upon yourself. Your unnatural obsession with something as transient as a mere novel which far fewer people have read than you imagine (that's new, he used to proclaim both its worth and its popularity), your misplaced belief that you and I are cruelly lampooned in it, have turned me into an object of general pity and scorn to a far severer degree than any assumed malice on the part of the innocent author. It is *you*, your behaviour, which has drawn attention upon us and brought me to ridicule. Had you not proclaimed these supposed portrayals no one would have noticed them, although I continue to insist that they do not exist. (His logic is almost as lucid as mine.) Further I would recall to what ordered memory you may still possess my letter of fourteen days ago in which I informed you that I had been advised by one learned in law and close to the King that I may in all legality be rid of you, that there is sufficient instance and cause to annul our marriage upon the grounds of persistent insanity, *per causam lunaticae cronicae,* and yet I still hold off from this course while there is any hope of cure. Help me, I beg you, to prove my faith in this. (Ha! He's written like someone faintly human for the first time!) It is so slight a thing which you have puffed to such enormity for yourself and me. Please consult your chaplain, submit to be directed by him and pray continually to your Ultimate Judge so you be not cast into that Limbo which surely awaits those who know neither the world in its reality nor God in His mercy. I kiss your hands, from our house by the river to which I wish to see you restored, your sorely tried husband, et cetera. Scuttle, scuttle and the sparrow's eye is looking at me from beside the prayer stool. He crept out like a mouse. I look at him, get up from my chair, open the window and stand to one side. His head cocks, what is this huge being doing? Now he's flown at the window, hit the mullion, fallen to the sill! Fly, mouse bird, fly, the window's open.

At last he did, plummeting, fluttering, swooping, I thought he'd hurt his wings but no, he recovered his use of them just in time and he's gone now. Can I learn from such a sparrow? Or should I learn from between the lines of Jerónimo's letter? I began copying it out on a flood of hurt but by the end it was I who felt sorry for him. Perhaps he means what he can't express? But I won't, can't pray with the peg-doll chaplain, suppose the sun came out? And I've tried praying without him. Innocent author? Impossible. No one as perceptive as he was can be innocent. That's for children and the born stupid. Innocent Jerónimo? Well, yes, perhaps, that innermost bit of him, that shining core of real bewilderment, yes.

Later. I've suddenly seen my private sitting room in my house by the river, seen it in my mind in all its beautiful privacy, comfort, as it was that afternoon eight years ago when I'd invited the famous author to talk to me for the first time. I can't sleep in the afternoons, hardly at any time, I never drink wine during the day unlike Jerónimo who has a passion for the sweet, golden wines of Jerez de la Frontera and for tobacco, too, now, he leaves his used pipes everywhere, his afternoons are decimated by volleys of snorings he himself cannot hear. Thank God his rooms are on the other side of the main staircase from mine. And by the way, while my mind still circles, it isn't *our* house by the river as my husband wrote at the end of his letter. He was trying, I think, delicately for him, to imply an intimacy, sharedness which I know now can never be restored between us. Did it ever exist? I was so young when we were betrothed and he was so big-boned, a foot taller than me, where am I? The house, yes. It is mine, my house. I possess it absolutely, in law,[1] in fact, and in my imagination, too, in my love for it, and Jerónimo knows as well as I do that it was not, never was, part of my enormous dowry which he needed so badly; he is welcome to the rest of the loot I brought with me. Loot describes it exactly. My father imported hundreds of tons of gold and silver from the new world, some legally, which went after deduction of expenses to the crown, but even more illegally. There was a family joke about the whole dried leg of an Aztec being found in one sack, cut off at the hip for the sake of the gold bangle at the ankle. Father used to say he was in imports and exports but his wink made it clear it was mostly imports. Had he brought in less he would have been a common smuggler. I loved him dearly. In old age he became very dignified, he's buried beside my mother in the family mausoleum which was designed by an Italian architect almost as crooked as his patron. It's built of Carrara marble from Huesca. My father paid through the nose for his ponderous tomb but the house by the river was built before I was born when he was a simpler man less glutted by wealth.

My room there is high and cool overlooking gardens in the intricate Italian style. Beyond walls and pleached lime trees meadows lead down to the river. From my windows you can glimpse the water between the trunks of the poplars. We had an old pet camel which used to graze with the cows but he died a few years ago, about the same time the King or rather his hatchet man re-

[1] Surely María Isabel is mistaken? Even if the house was not included in the marriage settlement a wife's possessions became her husband's absolutely, documented or not.

patriated the Moors.[1] I think Ramadan died in sympathy, knowing like them that his only home was here. He had a floppy hump. My house has lovely wooden ceilings made by Moorish carpenters. Jerónimo was all for having our old camel stuffed and placed in the dining hall, it'll make our guests laugh, Maribel, but I said I would never be able to eat with Ramadan looking at me and for once he listened. I must stop circling but so many things lead to others, I don't think I shall ever see my room down there in the valley again.

Juana has just brought in my lunch and there is lettuce in a bowl, green, crisp lettuce. Really! That's typical of Jerónimo, really. To tell me off on the one hand and then from behind his back produce what I want with the other. Really! I almost didn't eat it, I almost threw it out of the window in a spat as Juana would say, but I have now and it was delicious. He must have sent at least to Valencia for it.

I'm feeling much better, much, and I think I might even describe him with a clear mind, our guest, I mean.

He came into my room sideways, that second day after his arrival. I hadn't seen him since our first dinner when Father Gattinara behaved so abominably. He sidled in, bowing twice and apparently embarrassed. I asked, was anything wrong, and he smiled knowing I was more nervous of this encounter than he was. I said, why did you come in so awkwardly? He pointed to his stocking behind the knee. A wide ladder ran down the plump white calf. Oh, dear, I said, haven't you got any others? He said, no, these were my best, my last pair suitable for such an interview, madam. I laughed. Surely a literary lion can afford stockings? He smiled gently. Madam, money runs from me as from a ghost, and there was a sudden chillness in the room in which I shivered. But his smile remained, presiding

[1] The Duke of Lerma, chief administrator to Philip III. Sixty-four thousand *Moriscos*, Moors who had been forcibly converted to Christianity, were expelled from Aragón in 1610.

over his explanation of how he'd caught his buckle in his stocking while dressing for what he called this privileged audience but his eyes were watchful. Why are you laughing at me? I said, disconcerted. I'm not, he said, I'm laughing at myself, and I believed him. He'd wanted to look his best, he'd dressed especially carefully even though realising as he did the impossibility, absurdity, unlikelihood of a man of his age impressing a beautiful young lady such as myself. He'd suffered a young man's agonies on the way up to my apartment, he said, heard the superior giggle of my observant lady-in-waiting behind him on the stairs. He distrusted ladies-in-waiting, he told me later. We laughed and laughed as he described his pretensions, delusions, so accurately, with such mocking detachment. Fancy a trifle like a laddered stocking upsetting a mature, acclaimed author, I said. That is the tyranny of beauty, madam, and vanity like poverty has no age limit, believe me. I promised him new stockings. I had twelve pairs of silk laid out in his room the next day. They were every colour of the rainbow. He wore them with joy, they became a private joke between us in the sun-flecked, shade-dappled days which followed. I couldn't talk to him enough, I sent for him every afternoon. Jerónimo indulged me, I'm sure you must have a secret passion for this funny little man, Maribel. Everyone looks small to Jerónimo. But then he is big and powerful and so always has lots of little men to do lots of large things for him.

But how did he really look, my enchanter? Jerónimo was almost right about him, he certainly wasn't tall but then neither was he a dwarf. He was medium. Round-shouldered with a neat pot-belly, the kind of apple plumpness which builds up surreptitiously on a man who is always thought of as slim by those who remember him when he was younger. He had auburn hair greying and receding at both temples, a rather surprisingly military-looking silver beard and moustache, long ears echoing the shape of his nose, bad teeth in a small mouth, he'd had a lot removed in Algiers years

26

before, he said. I asked him several times about his stay in Algiers but he always waved the question aside. His eyes were decidedly strange, contradictory. They were deeply set, hooded by heavy lids. The cast of them was somehow sad but at once you forgot this because of their brightness and the directness of their look. Someone or something was looking out of a cave at you and laughing without blinking. Oh, dear, he's fading, disappearing, waving goodbye as I describe him, or so it seems to me. Come back, please come back as you used to be. His eyes were the most important thing about him. I've already written (where are you?) how, when he chose, his eyes could make you feel you were the most interesting person in the world. They seemed to caress your whole spirit, essence, to create a better you and to elicit confidences you never thought you'd utter to anyone and after you'd spoken so freely, too freely, he'd nod and you'd feel, here at last is someone who understands; then the eyelids would drop.

Almost equally surprising was his skin. I mean the smoothness of it. In spite of time, he must have been sixty at least, his forehead and cheeks hadn't a wrinkle though at the corners of his eyes there were dozens of tiny ones. I've never seen such a generally baby-smooth face in someone of that age. It was so untroubled. It was as though he had washed each day's pain and difficulties away. His left hand was permanently crippled, it was like a buzzard's claw. It's no use, I can't give my real idea of him. He's gone, smiling.

He was scrupulously clean and never seemed to perspire. Inside him was bounce. It appeared that the world was still brand new to him, he could look at it as if it had never happened before so if you were with him you started to see it like that, too. I've never been so happy as when I saw the world again through his eyes because what he saw he liked, found extraordinarily, exceptionally, incredibly interesting, and at first I kept thinking it can't be, it isn't, it wasn't interesting before you came here so it can't be now, it's a trick, but it wasn't and quite soon I found I could see it as he did. The experience was like becoming a child again of course, but a very wise child hand in hand with this marvellous older one. I'm sure the pair of us became insufferable in our conspiracy of knowing innocence, we must have been horribly cloying to the outsider. I do remember as the first weeks of his visit went by that Jerónimo began to frown rather and his jokes became sourer. Maribel's Dutch uncle he used to call him to our friends. But that was later, our complicit innocence, I mean. We didn't begin that afternoon like that at all. I was awful but then so was he.

I asked him about his crippled hand which was a mistake because I received a long, boring account of an old sea-battle which he'd obviously told too many times. He had been astonishingly brave, had insisted on manning a par-ticularly dangerous post even though he was ill with dysentery and, well, I yawned. You don't like old soldiers' reminiscences, madam? No, I don't! I was really snappish. I liked your story of your stockings but people killing each other remind me of my husband who's always recounting his exploits in the Low Countries, his gallantry both on and off the battlefield burgeons at each retelling. He smiled politely at my petulance. I sighed. Silence. An itch between my shoulder blades, the buzz of a fly. I called my third chambermaid and ordered her to get rid of it. She galloped round the room with the fly-whisk, a fat girl desperate to please. My small world goes wrong very quickly. I dis-missed her telling her she was hopeless. He sat very still.

What does interest you, madam? he asked as the door closed and the fly began to buzz again. I didn't know how to answer, I didn't know him well enough to be truthful, to say, very little, almost nothing, I always seem to be waiting for something, I like this house but hardly any-where else, a book occasionally beguiles me, yours did, new clothes sometimes revive me, I'm very rich or rather I enjoy the wealth I brought my husband, I'm spoilt, I suppose, I don't do anything, I don't even produce children, not that I want children. No, I said none of that and I'm glad I didn't because I'd behaved badly enough already. Instead I laughed gaily, how my voice tinkled, and said I was utterly fascinated by literature, by poetry, by writing, which wasn't true at all, it was the sort of thing you say, I say, floundering at receptions when your host introduces you, me, to some uneasy semi-gentleman saying this is Sir So-and-So whose sonnets you must have read and you haven't, I haven't ever. What I really don't understand, what is an enigma to me, I said, is how anyone actually *begins* to write a poem or a play let alone an enormous book like yours, where *do* you get your ideas from? He seemed to take my idiot questions seriously but absorbed them with a sigh. I suppose you're always being asked that? I said. He agreed. And almost always by women. Men tend to take it for granted that the profession of letters is like any other, which it isn't. Why not? Why did I still sound so sharp? I could feel myself sprouting little knives all over, surely he could see them glinting in the slats of sun through the half-closed shutters. Why not what? Do you mean why is it a profession different from others, or why do women always question authors more freely than men do? Both, I said, and don't sound like a schoolmaster, please, I invited you here to amuse me. He sighed again, but his patience seemed limitless. Had I been him faced by me I should have bowed and left the room. I was trying to find out what you wanted to know, madam? Perhaps you don't really? I do, I do! I insisted, please don't tease me. Well, first, for most professions, madam, there's a period of training before you're allowed to profess whatever it is, medicine, law—I know that! I said. He said, of course, but please, we must go gently, softly towards what we are really talking about, don't you think? I agree I talk in simplicities but I am not condescending or teasing, madam, believe me, I like to make things as simple and clear as possible to begin with. His voice was quiet, peaceable if that's a word. I pouted, felt admonished but less edged somehow. But with writing, madam, you just begin, no one trains you except yourself, no one allows you to profess. An author has to learn everything as he begins and after he has begun or so I've found. And it doesn't matter whether he has a success at the beginning, in the middle, at the end or never at all, everything always remains to be learned. It is not a profession you can ever be prepared for, indeed for most authors it isn't a profession at all since they cannot live by writing. Few do, I haven't. For instance I am one of the least successful playwrights in Spain.[1] Clearly nature didn't intend me to write plays, it is a very particular ability, but still I continue to try and I'm very jealous of those who can write for the theatre, who hear the laughter and those heart-stopping silences when the audience dare not breathe from sheer expectation of delight or fear, and then the earthquake of applause and the parties enjoyed or not afterwards and the rehearsals before and the companionship, togetherness, and tantrums, not to mention the glorious flattery a playwright always receives from those curiously warm people, the actors, whose love and loyalty are as unfathomable as the most seasonal pond. How I long for that, how I long to belong. Writing novels you need never see anyone for months or years. And you don't. But doesn't a writer learn from other authors, from the classics? I thought I was sounding more sensible, more controlled but my face was cricking into another yawn which I didn't want him to see because I wasn't quite so bored or impatient as I had been. I hid it with my fan, well, I hope I did. Oh, yes, he said, one can read them, one must, I do. I read everything and anything which comes to hand, Ovid, the grocery bill I can't pay this week, announcements for the buying of land in the Americas, journals, romances, anything. But when I sit

[1] Untrue, Cervantes enjoyed some real, if limited, success in the theatre before being superseded by Lope de Vega, that 'monster of nature' as he calls him in the introduction to his collection of short plays or Interludes, known as *Los Entremeses*.

down to write nothing I've read can help me, indeed the greater the author the more mysterious are his methods. But you can imitate, surely? Oh, yes, but that isn't real writing, is it? Indeed it's possible to imitate what you haven't even read which can be rather a disappointment when you discover it and that is why I read everything I can. He laughed. When you write, madam, it is as if writing writes you, yourself. I'm sorry, I don't understand, except it sounds more complicated and sadder than I thought, I said. But it was I who felt sad and complicated. I thought you would be as jolly as your book, I said. I think, indeed I know, madam, that you would understand if you were to try to write. Me? Don't be stupid, what have I to say? Most people have one thing to say. Many authors spin that one thing out till doomsday. Are you happy when you write? Wholly happy however difficult it is and it's often unbelievably easy. I have a facility which amazes me, that's when I tear it up next day. So nothing's certain ever? I said and got up. He got up too. No, sit down, please, I said. He sat again so quickly it was almost comic. And why do women question you more than men? Because women, leisured women like yourself, madam, are more curious, I often find, more speculative. Are we? What are we interested in? Being, the world, what is real, what is not. For men existence is an arena to perform in so they have less inclination to question it. Some do, of course, but most don't. If a soldier wonders about the true nature of his enemy, the enemy becomes more difficult to kill in direct proportion to his understanding of him, so soldiers stick to labels like unbeliever, traitor, Indian. But you write about men, not women, your heroes are men, so you must find men more interesting than women? He said, I often think of them as a married couple, especially in this second book I'm writing. You're writing a sequel? How lovely! I hope so. When will it be finished? I don't know. I make no promises even to myself. Why do you think of them as married? Because each needs the other to confirm his

31

identity and actions. Male and female attributes flicker and fluctuate between them and they talk all the time, I can't stop them talking, especially Sancho, he's prepared to gobble up the world now and talk about it with his mouth full. But they're just master and servant really, aren't they? Yes, married, as I said, he answered. You always talk in opposites, I said, everything is a paradox, I think it's an easy way of sounding clever, don't you? No reply. The hint of a shrug in his shoulders. Silence. I'd wanted badly to feel victorious but I didn't.

I believe we've talked enough, madam, he said. Not at all, I lied brightly, do stay, (he'd got up again), I find our conversation mesmerising, I was panicking, I didn't seem to like him after all but I didn't want him to go, I get so lonely, I said, I never have anyone to really talk to, you are quite wrong about married people talking to each other all the time, they don't, Jerónimo and I don't. I was married at nine and I've never yet spoken to him properly, never! And I'm not interested in the world! You don't know anything, you just say you do, you invent anything and say it's true, I found myself shouting. The door opened and my second lady-in-waiting, I had so many then and Jerónimo seduced every one, looked in anxiously, are you all right, madam? Go away, I screamed at her, go away, I'm talking to the wisest man in the world, what he says is so simple it must be clever, why do you watch me all the time? Go away! She went. I'm sorry, I said, but this house is full of spies, they work for my husband, his eyes are everywhere, in every stuffed head on the stairs.

Your marriage was arranged, of course? he asked as if nothing had happened, as if my face hadn't splintered into noise, as if my lady-in-waiting hadn't snapped out of the door like a jack-in-the-box, as if the room hadn't swollen like a soap bubble and then fanned into a peacock's tail of iridescent jelly full of shining eyes. I was shaking, every part of my body trembling but I wasn't crying yet, I was panting and between each tearing breath I knew I would

32

soon hear my voice, small and clear, coming from a little alabaster statue of Diana I'm very fond of which stood on a pedestal behind him. I could see her perched on his left shoulder but, thank God, he didn't turn to speak to her, if he had I'd have disappeared, he kept looking at me and Diana was saying for me in a voice of crystalline composure, yes, Jerónimo needed my money and I needed his title my father said, he was eight years older than me when we were betrothed but now he's many years more, I don't know how many, not as many as you, but many, but I wasn't like this then, not at nine years old. I was excitable, nervous, María Isabel is highly strung was the family phrase for me, and Jerónimo went away after the ceremony, straightaway he went away, and I still lived at home with my dolls and my pets as if nothing had happened except dressing up for a game in the family chapel to which the Archbishop of Zaragoza came specially, such an honour for the family, María Isabel, it's because your husband's family is so old and so noble, my mother told me, and he's gone now to fight for you and Spain, he's a captain of horse in Holland, I'll get your father to show you a map and I looked at the map but I couldn't see my husband in name anywhere so I put him from my mind because I was petrified of him. He had a voice like a gong. He didn't come back for six years but when he did he was huger and hairier with a moustache and I knew he was going to devour me alive but I didn't tell that to anyone. He took me to Valladolid because the court had just moved there and my father owned a house in the city, my father turned so much of his money into stone, and there were receptions and parties and balls every night and fireworks and bullfights and Jerónimo became a bullfighter with a long spear and the horses he rode screamed like I scream when I'm unwell and everybody told me how brave he was leaning over the bull all four feet of his horse off the ground and his spear skewered into the hump of the bull behind the horns which were now lost inside the stomach of the horse and we'd all leapt to our feet shouting Jerónimo, brave Jerónimo! And we went everywhere together, what a delightful couple, people said, the bride so tiny, the groom such a man, such a muscular man but they didn't know his weight as I knew his weight. My parents were always there, too, except when we retired to our bed, that field of nightmare, and thanks to my giant husband they met everyone who mattered and they were so proud of me for buying them all the noble introductions my mother had ever dreamed of, my mother who had been a haberdasher's daughter from Pamplona. My voice had come back to me, was mine again.

It's grown dark while I've been writing and my wrist aches as it did that day when he found us hawking by the river but it's an ache I prefer. Juana's come in to make up the fire and to wash me. She says she won't take no for an answer this time. She's lit the candles, told me off for hurting my eyes with all this scritch-scratching as she calls it and made this stone box more cosy, more comfortable in five minutes than I could in five days. I stand facing the fire (I'm writing this before mass today, Sunday, in gratitude) and I let her unlace my dress, my petticoats. Her knobbly hands are kind, her voice rough. Now she takes the sponge and washes my back, buttocks, legs, tut-tuts at the scars on my thighs, you munna allow the doctor to open 'em again, Miss Maribel, she says, sponging the front of me firmly, you'll be skin and bone at this road, I've known you plumper, and then she drapes a towel round me and I hug it to me and feel nicer, better even than I did after eating the lettuce. And as she puts the towel on me she kisses my neck quickly, she always does that every night, you mun eat your supper in bed, do you hear? And I say, yes, Juana, I will, thank you and she squints up at me and says there's nowt so daft as folks so dunna believe 'em, Miss

Maribel![1] And I tell her I won't, I promise, I'll only ever believe what she tells me and after I've eaten my bean soup and she's drawn the curtains on each side of the bed but left the end ones open so I can see the fire I sleep and I dream of a courtyard and an old dog asleep in the sun, nothing else.

Sunday proper 30th January

After mass with the peg doll. Outside silver rain, bits of sun, pretend April. Inside, me. The room tidy, swept while I was in the chapel, Juana always gets what she wants and you're glad, really. Mass seemed never ending, but although my knees grew numb with kneeling, the chaplain couldn't stop my eyes enjoying another place so I feel refreshed even if I did have to take communion from his hands. He has the kind of pastry flesh which if you touch it accidentally — I'd never touch him voluntarily even though he is a man of God, no more than I'd touch those puff-balls you find in the fields on October mornings — the kind of flesh which records the dent, has no resilience, does not spring back into place, oh, how I wish I could write the sound my repugnance makes in my throat. I choked on the wine, those hands on the chalice, and I coughed on the wafer, thank God he offered it in a napkin. It is not that I'm a secret atheist, it's just that I can't bear him, the peg doll. Our old chaplain who died last year was bad enough, pompous, opinionated, but this one exudes such familiarity with God you feel he sees Him in his mirror every morning. He can't be much older than I am, perhaps two or three years though it's difficult to tell, his manners are so smooth. He wears his dead mother's wedding ring on his little finger. When mass was finally over and I was able to rise at last I said,

---

[1] The Duchess records her maid's speech in the dialect of north-western Spain. I have attempted an equivalent in English which conveys something of the tone of the original.

thank you, chaplain, you sang all three anthems beautifully, how do you manage it without accompaniment? I have perfect pitch, madam, he said with a smile like cow-heel glue. As we left the chapel and climbed the stairs, the sun came out and there was his shadow on the wall and I swayed, nearly fainted, he put out a helpful hand, that brought me to my senses and I ran up ahead of him shouting, thank you, father, thank you, father, thank you. But there was no escape, he followed me in here. There is one other thing, madam. What? And he said he had prepared a new programme of reformation for me which has been approved by my husband in name and which will prepare me to enter a barefoot sisterhood for distressed gentlewomen in the mountains behind here. We are to begin his regime tomorrow morning at ten o'clock. I shall find it spiritually beneficial. Is that why Jerónimo sent the lettuce? I asked. I don't understand, madam? As a bribe, I said, to me. Still he didn't understand. No, of course, you wouldn't, I said, good day, chaplain. He quarter bowed and left. His bow is beautifully judged, it acknowledges my precarious status perfectly, allowing me just enough respect but no more. It is an obeisance to the shell of me.

I was in the company of my distinguished author when Juana came in last night and put me to bed and I slept as I haven't slept for five weeks and now I feel more in command of myself, I think, except for certain things like just now on the stairs. I feel as if there could be some sort of resistance in me provided no one tests my new-found determination too hard. Barefoot sisterhood? I shall tell the chaplain it is he who should join a bare-arsed brotherhood, that's what I shall say! No, I mustn't translate my anger into bravado, here on this page, no, or I won't have any left for him tomorrow. No, I must let the peg doll wait.

That other room where I was happy, well, where I felt safe, where the shutters are pushed back again because the sun has moved round. I know it is correct now to say that the earth has moved round but to me, to my feelings, to my experience, it is still the sun which moves, I can't help it, I observe the stars from what I still feel to be a fixed point despite what my mind accepts from the new philosophers. And while the earth moves how is it they hold their telescopes steady? Perhaps there are two kinds of motion, of the head and of the heart? The sun still shines on the knot gardens and the meadows, but slantingly, the shadows of the poplars are on the river now. I must turn back the pages of this book to where I was yesterday.[1]

Yes, my voice had just returned to me from the little statue of Diana which had seemed to perch on his shoulder. But I can't remember what he did or said then. It's a long time ago, of course, eight years at least, but I thought I'd never forget anything about him, but I have. *I must* know what he did or said, I must. No. Gone. Gone.

Monday 31st January

I've put off the peg doll with a pretend chill. I don't want to get up. I don't want to write anything. I hate everybody.

Tuesday 1st February

Pinch, punch, first day of the month and no returns![2]

Wednesday 2nd February

I've now got the chill I pretended to have on Monday.

---

[1] The MS is in loose-leaf form but there is evidence that it was originally a book. There are needle holes and vestiges of gum. Cf. the entry for Friday 4th February 1616, page 58.

[2] The original reads: *El golpe de la sartén aunque no duele tizna.* This proverb does not translate easily. I have therefore tried to match María Isabel's inchoate rebelliousness with this childish incantation.

I'm writing this in bed. It is awkward. My head throbs. It's snowing outside. What will I do tomorrow when the doctor comes? Juana is right. This time I must refuse, resist. I must. Oh, my head.

Thursday 3rd February

There's going to be a tremendous fuss. I'm sure he still doesn't believe it. I'm not sure I do. I simply said no with unfathomable calm, undeniable dignity even, for me. I didn't start trembling, I'm almost laughing as I write, I can't put the words down fast enough, such a triumph, my face and neck didn't get hot, I had no sudden shortness of breath, nor did my voice come from anywhere but from me, from the place where I stood. I'm terrifically proud of myself. I behaved as untroubled people do, for once.

Juana ushered him in. I allowed him to unpack his leather bag of all its unspeakable instruments, let him talk, he's juicily proud of his rich brown voice is Dr Villanueva. And how is our ladyship feeling today? Recovered from her chill, I hear? And he looked up at me with his squashed raspberry nose which can scarcely support the weight of his spectacles, he's ridiculously short-sighted, his pale blue eyes swim behind glass thick as the base of medicine bottles. Is that what they're made of? He is a circumspect, thrifty person. It's rumoured he has amassed a fortune but he certainly doesn't wear it on his back. He has dandruff, too. Why are all the people Jerónimo appoints for my well-being so physically repellent to me? Perhaps they're not, really? Perhaps I see them through spectacles as distorting as Dr Villanueva's? But this time I did not allow his presence or appearance to panic me. It was wonderful. I said my chill was a temporary indisposition, some catarrh remained, my nose smelt and felt as if it were full of stringy onions but generally I was much more myself because the Duke, my husband, had

38

recently answered my plea for more salad in my diet. He nodded perfunctorily. I always have the feeling that he never really listens to me but this morning I was determined he would. He agreed that diet was important, so he had heard me! There must already have been something in my manner which commanded attention! Indeed he said he'd been present when the chaplain had reported my request to his lordship and had supported it on two grounds, one of digestive variety, the other of indulgence since, in his view, such harmless whims of a disordered mind were better assented to than refused. They were not pertinent to a cure, however. I thanked him coolly, deflecting his professional smile with another of my own. I suddenly felt I had a profession, too! Of untouchable gentility. And now, he said, if her ladyship would be so gracious as to recline herself upon the bed we may proceed to the purpose of my visit. And, of course, that was when I refused. I swear his ears wriggled with the effort to receive the information. I was about to laugh but such was my new-found control I didn't. Juana, by the fire heating the water, gawped. I said, I refuse your treatment, doctor, I refuse it. My treatment, madam? He no longer called me your ladyship. It is not my treatment, madam, it is yours, as ordered by your lord, your husband. Who? I said. The Duke, who else? And while I am delighted to hear that you consider your condition improved I should hope my opinion might carry more weight, it will with the Duke, your husband. Who? I said. He no longer heard me. And my opinion is, madam, that at this very moment, as I observe the dilation of the pupil in the iris (he peered at me bottle-eyed) you are gravely disturbed and grievously requiring relief from the pressure of black blood—You're mistaken, I interrupted, you judge me by yourself, look at your nose, doctor! And I gathered up his surgical tools, flung them higgledy-piggledy into his bag and with sinuous composure handed it graciously to him. Good morning, Dr Villanueva, I no longer require your services, I find your appearance distasteful, your manner overbearing, your competence questionable, you've been treating me for far too long, I have been lacerated by your attentions, and I am still as I am. I shall report your conduct, madam, he blustered. I did nearly break in two then. I very nearly did stamp and scream, of course you will, you quack, you spy, but something saved me from fragmenting and I was able to say, please do, do please, tell my husband in name how much better I am. He did not bow before he went. I shut the door behind him. I'd have liked to have locked it but I think the chaplain took the key on Tuesday. I haven't proof he did but on Tuesday it was there and on Wednesday it wasn't. Juana is convinced he took it. She stared at me, there were tears in her eyes, then she jumped up and down with joy. Oh, Miss Maribel, she said, that was champion!

No one has come. It's more than an hour ago since I watched him ride off from my window. He's got a terrible seat, his green velvet bottom bounces on his poor horse like a watermelon. What can he have said to the peg doll? We were due to begin my postponed course of instruction at eleven o'clock and the courtyard clock has already chimed twelve. This despite my protests that after the doctor's attentions I would need to rest. I said that to him even though I knew I was going to refuse the doctor. A lie! I was able to lie, so I *must* be better!

I still feel pleased with myself but not quite so elated as I was, my victory's wearing thin because now I keep thinking of what I daren't, which is how Jerónimo will take the news of my rebellion from the raspberry-nosed watermelon. Oh, God, there's a knock at the unlocked door and it's opening before I've said come in and the sun's come out, oh, God!

Four o'clock. I go for days, cold days when nothing happens and then some things are crushed into one whole day, box, me. I can't write about it yet, no. Men are such

40

fearsome creations even when they've chosen not to be men as such or rather especially when they've embraced God or the Church or whatever it is which awards them yet more power, more authority, and I've suddenly seen Jerónimo's family portraits which he brought from Caparroso to hang in rows in my house by the river, the male heads like suns bursting on white plates, the armoured stomachs like the prows of fighting ships, the steel fists gripping batons or scrolls like batons, the chains of office, the eyes fixing you, going through you, the turned faces blank with sheer ownership, the legs, however woodenly depicted, leaping out of the darkness at you. But my author wasn't like that, especially not his legs in the stockings I'd given him. I remember some days by the colour of his calves. He seemed to me to be too pleased with them. Or did his pleasure and vanity suggest one should delight in the smallest things as they occur? As I did the lettuce, which in a way was the foundation of my rebellion?

My next memory is of us walking by the river and he was calling me Maribel, so I must have told him he could, so he must have won my trust. But how, when we started off so badly? I don't know. Perhaps because he tolerated my talking? He certainly had a kind of patience which in anyone else would have been frightening. Anyway, he was calling me Maribel and I was glad because there had been a terror for me in his earlier politeness, formality. He hadn't been in any way subservient, he'd simply observed the social proprieties so, so punctiliously I felt there had to be some kind of mockery of me underneath. I think now I was wrong, that there wasn't any, not then, no, he was reserving his real derision for later. I ought really to cross out that last sentence but I can't, my hand won't do it. In future, however, I shall discipline myself to record those days in their innocence otherwise I won't have anything to counterweight what I now know of him. His charm, his treachery.

41

We were walking along the bank beside the trees and he was telling me—the air from the water was cooler than the air in the meadows where he had admired Ramadan—he was telling me a story about a young man, a student he'd known in Rome, who had thought he was made of glass and would break if he was jostled or fell over.[1] I felt calm and sensible, walking with balance, a straight back and everything I saw was exactly what it was, neither too big nor too small, nor too near nor too far, everything in creation was in its right place, quite delicious, and irradiated by the summer sun. We stopped to watch a heron near the bank. We watched it without speaking for five minutes in which time, the heron's time, nothing about it moved except the elegant head with its spear beak and tucked down plume. What infinite poise it had as it quartered the shallows for fish. It caught nothing. Eventually it waded away amidst suddenly darting water boatmen. I'm always interested in delusions, dementia, he said. I've visited the asylums of Madrid, Seville, Milan and Córdoba and if you would like my opinion, Maribel, oh, yes, I would, please, I said and my skimming laugh took only one, two, three skips to cross that wide, golden river. Well, he said, although you've told me, twice now (had I, when was the other time?), that you think sometimes you must be going mad, I do not think you are or need be. I don't know why I believe you, I answered too quickly, because my husband says the same and I don't believe him so why should I you? Well, that might be because you didn't let me finish. Oh? What? What were you going to say which would make so great a difference? I hope it will, Maribel. What I was about to say was that I don't think you are mad but you could become mad if you don't tell someone. Tell them what? I felt a prickle of panic. I'm a very good listener,

[1] It would seem that the Duchess had not read Cervantes's *Exemplary Novels* published in 1613 in which there is a story called 'El Licenciado Vidriera' best translated as 'The Glass Graduate'.

Maribel, you may say whatever you like to me, I shan't tell a soul, I promise. Tell them what? I don't know, whatever you wish about yourself. Are you some sort of doctor? He laughed. No, nor a priest, I'm more a receptacle for human follies. You sound too good to be true, I said. We were in the hot meadows again. Or if you cannot bring yourself to talk to me you might keep a diary, write down everything you think and feel and think you feel. Is that your answer to everything, to write? It's the only way I know. Only way what? Why do you never explain? You don't, do you, ever? You talk, you laugh, you tell amusing stories but never explain. He sighed. I do explain in the end but I have to go slowly because I'm not clever. What nonsense! It's true, Maribel, I'm no wiser than you, only older which isn't the same thing, but I have found, and perhaps this only applies to me, that when you write you put yourself as someone else over there in a landscape and the landscape is you, too. In this way you become not only another person but also another object which moves in time and space and even if you're quite lunatic and doing inexplicable things like going mad for love or turning cartwheels because you think you are a cartwheel, you're still an object over there which you can look at. And if you can look from a distance however short then you can understand and if you can understand then you are not mad. I said, but that's what I do and it's not like that at all! I often see myself over there when I have one of my tantrums as Jerónimo calls them, that's how I know I'm not myself in fact when I do see myself, feel myself going over there, that's when, that's when I know I won't be able to stop that other me, which is me, from doing the most awful things, from saying the most awful things. And the person who is watching all this commotion, who is she? Me, of course, in agonies. And when the fit passes you come together again, the here you and the there you? Yes, yes, I do, and it's all right again, I'm whole again so if I were to write

43

about me I'd be deliberately putting myself where I hate being, actually encouraging myself to have that two-people feeling I'm so frightened of, wouldn't I? I bit my lip, I could feel the itch between my shoulders, the shortness of breath which always signals an attack, bright battle banners flapping on lances. Please, I panted, don't advise me again, I can't manage advice, I know I should but I can't. I can only listen to myself. I'm sorry if that sounds selfish, stupid, but it's true. I panic whenever people tell me things. He nodded and we walked on through the meadow and he trod in a cowpat and he was so funny as he examined his shoe that the banners furled themselves inside me and disappeared beyond the brow of a long hill, bright horizon, somewhere in my head and I knew there would be no more calls to battle that day. I still don't know if it was accident or if he did it to distract me. Was it advertent or not?

Another day, another afternoon, he would never meet me in the mornings, he told me Jerónimo had invited him to go hawking. Will you go? I should like to refuse. He'll be offended, he's very proud of his hawks, they confirm his pedigree. Have you seen his collection? He has them sent from all over Europe, he has peregrines from Scotland, falcons from France, even a goshawk from Bavaria. When they die he has them stuffed. He trains them himself. Yes, we looked round the mews. I'll go, Maribel, if you go. No, I won't, I shall never go hawking again. My first sight of you was with a hawk on your wrist. I know. You looked wonderful. All right, I won't go, I shall risk offending the Duke. You'd better not stay till September, that's when the real hunting begins. I presume you don't like hunting? No, although I'm quite happy for others to do it for me, I like eating game, and it keeps our warriors in battle-readiness, I daresay. Jerónimo says that. I'm sure he does, it's what hunters always say. If you stay you'll find we go up to our hunting lodge in the hills. It's a day's ride from here. Jerónimo had it built three years ago, it's a sort of miniature barracks. It's made of stone with a courtyard. It even has a pretend portcullis. It's a cold, angular, echoey place. I hate it. He invites all our neighbours, the flowers of Aragón they're known as, and they set out each day, all the men and some of the women. They drive deer, wild boar, wolves, even the odd bear sometimes. Do you ride with them? I used to, when I believed my first duties were towards my husband, but now it is as much as I can manage to see their eyes when they come back, eyes shot through with the blood and light of the animals they've killed, it's as if they've absorbed all the life out of every wild creature. They have mule carts to haul back the corpses. Other times they take guns and shoot birds, even the smallest, they come back with hundreds of pitiful scraps hanging from their belts. They and I eat and drink for hours in the evenings, interminable dinners of inordinate ceremony punctuated by boasts, toasts, fanfares of hunting horns, rude songs. Next morning they're up before dawn with sour jokes, blurred faces, headaches to be ridden off, cursings of grooms, guffaws, fartings.

He said that he'd make good his escape before September and I wanted to say that I would come with him but naturally I didn't.

The next day he told me that Jerónimo had laughed loudly when he begged to be excused the hawking expedition. My dear fellow, I hardly expected you, an author, to join us, too much ink in your veins. His imitation of Jerónimo was exact and we both laughed at my husband's predictable joke before talking about poetry or did we? Was it that day we played that game, he said it was a version of an Arab one? I think it was. He would write a line of verse, we agreed the subject and metre before-hand, then he folded the paper so I couldn't see what he'd written, then I had to write a line, I was very nervous, and hand it back, folded over again. And so on, to and fro between us until he said we had written a sonnet. He then pulled out the concertina-ed paper and read it aloud. It was very peculiar, of course, because the lines didn't have much to do with each other but suddenly the last two lines did almost fit each other and that seemed nice. We laughed at our silly sonnet very happily. I remember the last couplet still. The subject was the power of love. The lines aren't exactly glowing from the mint of creation but they still chink a little. Time has dimmed them, of course.

There's None can say he has not felt his Power,
A Lover's minute is another's Hour.

And the time had disappeared between us because I remember being surprised when Marco came in. But you said five o'clock, my lady. Is it really five, good heavens? Marco had come to discuss the entertainments we were planning for the following week and since these were intended to be a surprise for our guest I had to ask him to leave. He went at once, vanishing with such quick tact I was left feeling deserted, wanting to say come back.

I discussed the masque for an hour. Marco had brought meticulously drawn sketches of the carts that were to appear in the grand procession, the whole thing was a procession really, and clearly they were going to be delightfully decorated. Our steward spared us no expense. Finally he worked round to his real request. The page who was to have played the part of Dulcinea was no longer suitable, he said. Why? His voice has broken during rehearsals, my lady. But won't that make it even funnier, a gawk of a boy with an erratic voice, squeak, boom, it'll be perfect, surely? Marco assumed a pained, professional man-of-the-theatre face mixed with a major-domo's deference, I hesitate to contradict you, my lady, but in this superior presentation of mine I wish the Princess Dulcinea to appear in her ideal, Platonic form. Oh, I said. Well, in that case you'd better ask one of my ladies-in-waiting, that new one who came last week is exceptionally pretty,

46

Jerónimo's already started pinching her bottom. He blushed at this indiscretion. I was not supposed to notice my husband's proclivities, infidelities, it was an unspoken rule of the house. Finally Marco coughed and came out with it. Would her ladyship consider playing the part? Me? I was truly surprised. Me, Marco? No, no, I couldn't, don't be ridiculous, I could never remember the lines. There are only ten, my lady. I realise it's a bold request but your beauty is without equal, it would be a *coup de théâtre* as the French say. I laughed, shaking my head. He begged me to think again, you would be perfect in the role, my lady. The pull of things theatrical is astonishing; despite myself I was thrown into breathless, exquisite turmoil by a smoothly ambitious steward requesting my appearance in a home-made pageant! No, to be fair to myself, it was more than that, it was the thought both tempting and frightening of appearing before my author as one of his creations and not in Dulcinea's peasant body either, but as the ideal, the unchallengeable perfection, shining inside another's shell of being, inside his scarecrow knight's head and heart. How could I embody her? The next day I told Marco I would play the part.

I think I've recovered enough composure to record the chaplain's attempt to establish his new regime. I think. I'd like to put it off until tomorrow. But I don't know what will happen tomorrow, not after today.

He came in at one o'clock wearing a deadly expression of glistening rectitude. He made no mention of Dr Villanueva's visit. He was carrying a pile of books, necessary reading for me, a penitent's hood, required to be worn by me, and a sort of whip. He set these objects down as I shut this book, produced the missing key with a portentous flourish and locked the door. I said, so you did steal the key to my door, chaplain? It was as if I hadn't spoken. Another appointed saviour was deaf to me. He turned to face me, drew himself up to his full height, the room was full of snow-bright sun, his shadow lengthened, and I said, please remove your hat, please, but again he didn't hear me. No one does. My voice was faint, of course, by then. He began to speak, very quietly and so quickly I couldn't understand at first. When I did he was cursing me, efficiently employing overwhelming gusts of sacred abuse designed to cast out devils. I'm to be systematically blasted into sanity, blown over the hill and faraway upon the icy winds of God's home truths to appear purified at last, plonk, in the cloisters of that barefoot sisterhood where I shall no longer be an impediment to anyone. He spoke his soul-shrivelling exorcism so fast I cannot remember it all but the gist was I was full of pride which was so noxious that it reminded him of various unmentionable bodily functions which he proceeded to mention while his nose wrinkled at the smell of his own metaphors. My pride was hermaphroditic apparently, a double-ended devil continually in congress with itself, a wriggling ring of self-swallowing lust which quite disregarded the seasons of the flesh. Here he reached and sustained a crescendo of comparisons of such variegated filth that I wonder now, I couldn't at the time, if he was voicing things of more intimate concern to himself than to me? When he drew breath at last he ordered me, he was still shaking and sweating, he ordered me to read the passages he had marked in the books he'd brought and also, he drew himself to a yet higher height of rectitude, since I had improperly refused the prescribed medical attentions for my condition, physical chastisement must now go hand in hand with spiritual correction, he said. And he picked up the whip. I could scarcely speak but I did say, it was only a murmur, Dulcinea must be disenchanted? If he heard he didn't understand, like his predecessor he does not read novels. I thought I ought to explain, which was foolish, and anyway he cut me short, we must begin now, María Isabel! Can eyeballs perspire? Yes, his could.

I cannot easily describe the events which followed. He touched me, such horror, attempting to pull my dress from

48

my back. I almost fainted, his hand upon me, his shadow on the stone floor, I screamed and Juana was banging on the locked door, calling, Miss Maribel, Miss Maribel! We were struggling, he struck me with the whip, I kicked his shins, he tripped over the prayer stool and hit his head on a firedog. I thought I had killed him. Miss Maribel! Juana, I've killed him! The key, open the door, Miss Maribel! Somehow I took the key from his cassock. When Juana saw him she screamed so shrilly his eyes opened. He got clumsily to his feet and together Juana and I pushed that appalling man out of the room. I locked the door again. So now I've committed two crimes in one day. I'm sure he'll tell Jerónimo I tried to kill him even though his bang on the head was an accident.

Later and Juana's gone to find some food for me. I keep the key now. There's been absolute silence for hours. My hands have begun to shake every now and then and I have to stop writing until they stop. The peg doll hasn't left as the doctor did. If he had I should have seen him cross the courtyard to the stables. He could, of course, have left by the kitchens at the back, or sent someone else to report my behaviour, there are two mules kept for market and firewood in the barn. If he has gone or sent someone I'm sure my husband will come tomorrow to interview me. I don't think he would kill me, he could, of course, I'm sure the law would uphold him, I'm his property. I feel like a table which wobbles every time you try to use it in any way at all.

Midnight and I can't sleep for thinking. Juana came back at nine o'clock with bread and a small piece of cheese, the cook refused to supply anything more. She stayed with me till ten. She said she had spoken to no one but the cook and the chaplain's valet. Neither would tell her anything, pursed-lip silence. They take the peg doll's part against us, she says. She peeped into the chapel and saw him praying. So I'm in limbo on a restricted diet, held in a nowhere of unknown decisions either already

49

taken or about to be. I wonder who Jerónimo is snoring with tonight? I don't care, I just wonder. My candle's burning low and I haven't got another. Perhaps Juana can steal some more tomorrow? Oh, dear, my room is full of sputtering second thoughts: was I right to refuse the doctor, the chaplain? I thought I was, yes. But now? I don't know. Yes, no, yes. But how can I be sure? Who can I ask? There is only Juana but she loves me and always says I'm right whatever I do. Once she decides to love someone that person can do no wrong, ever, ever. Her loves and hates are as fixed as the earth still is to her. Anyway she's gone now. *He* would have known, of course. There it is, that's the last of the candle.

Friday 4th February

More sunshine after more snow in the night. I'm a prisoner obsessed by weather and time, especially now that the courtyard clock has stopped. I woke up in the night not hearing it. Has the chaplain had it stopped or is it a natural mechanical fault? I hope the latter because I prefer to be a victim of emblematic chance rather than considered deprivation. No one has arrived yet.

When I played the part of Dulcinea everyone applauded, especially him. Marco's masque was performed outside. It began at dusk. Summer storm clouds had gathered so there was a strange, baleful light which suited our play-acting perfectly. We had dined at five o'clock, forty of us in an extravagant silk-lined pavilion. Jerónimo loves entertaining in the open air; tents, picnics, stirrup-cup rituals make him feel like Genghis Khan. I hadn't told him, our guest, or Jerónimo, that I was taking part, so I had to make an excuse to slip away from the table to change into my costume. I don't think *he* believed me at all, he has a good nose for a lie. Jerónimo assumed I was my usual unwell self, of course.

It was a most elaborate pantomime. God knows what

magic Marco had used to prise the money out of my husband. As a prelude thick smoke was allowed to drift out of the trees beyond the lawn in front of the pavilion. The wind was in just the right direction. Marco has enormous luck although he always insists he has calculated everything. Had it been blowing from the south it would have engulfed our guests but our prevailing winds are westerly so perhaps Marco deserved his good fortune? He'd been very firm with Jerónimo about the siting of the pavilion. The smoke came from green bonfires which as they gathered heat and strength burst into flames, then explosions. Marco loves fireworks. At the first explosion, a trumpet fanfare rang out from the depths of the wood followed by drumming. The trumpets and the drums were joined by a roar of cannon and muskets. Marco believes in commanding his audience's attention. There were four volleys from the cannon, three from the muskets. The repeated noises were tremendous; from where I stood with my hands over my ears I could just glimpse the windows of the house shaking at the sound. Out of this disciplined military cacophony (in rehearsal Marco was no longer deferential but a martinet), out of this hullabaloo and echo appeared the figures of our honoured guest's two heroes miming flight from a field of battle. Marco played the knight and a fat kitchen boy the squire. He'd found a wonderfully woebegone horse for himself, all skin and bone, and, of course, a round-bellied donkey for the squire, neither kind of animal being in short supply in our nearest village. They had been meant to gallop out of the trees into the middle of the lawn but both animals refused in performance what they'd promised in rehearsal which was, I suppose, in character. But the actor playing Sancho Panza had the wit to jump off and pull hard while Marco shouted hoarsely at him to stand and face the enemy. Eventually they hauled their animals to their proper position in front of the pavilion and were able to adopt the attitudes required by their characters and

51

the story which was about to unfold: the knight absurdly fearless, the squire crouching in terror. This tableau was applauded. I wish I could have seen our guest's face at this impersonation but I was two hundred yards away in the wood, waiting for the cue to enter. He told me afterwards that he had found his heroes accurately portrayed but I suspect he was being diplomatic. There must have been some details which weren't right, some aspects which grated upon their originator, although, of course, he does say in the prologue to his novel that he is their stepfather, not their father. Is he admitting he stole the idea from someone else or is it his typical false modesty? I don't know. But I cannot believe we fleshed out his imagination to his complete satisfaction, there's always so much for the spectator to forgive in an amateur pantomime. And clearly, as his book reveals, he does not forgive.

The next actor to appear was dressed as a demon with a trumpet. In his fictionalised account he gives this demon a huge hollow ox-horn to blow, but in reality it was an ordinary trumpet, author's licence, I suppose, a heightening for effect. He embellishes so much that after a while you cannot tell where reality ends and fiction begins. He is unscrupulous, a ruthless Pizarro despoiling other people's worlds. The demon had a speech which he spoke quite well except for a lisp. Otherwise his voice was resonant, so deep and booming that it seemed not to belong to someone so short and broad. Strange contradictions in one personage. He was a groom. The speech was in rhyming couplets and its purpose was to announce the order of events to come. Who are you? shouted the squire. I am the Devil, was the answer, and I'm looking for a famous wandering knight known as Don Quixote. I am he, replied Marco with appropriate dignity, whereupon the Devil was launched on his slip-slop sea of couplets. I can't remember them now but the rhymes were so obvious everyone groaned in delight. The Devil heralded three wizards and his tumbling exit, lovely somersaults and handsprings, was the cue for the farm carts ahead of me to trundle out of the trees accompanied by more fanfares. The three carts were drawn by oxen with torches tied to their horns, another detail he remembered later. Each wizard on each cart wore a fantastic mask, necromantic robes and an outsize hat. The last one was meant to be an Arab enchanter-cum-historian calling himself Cide Hamete Benengeli, the supposed author of the first book of Don Quixote's adventures. It was a rather pedantic compliment to our guest which was probably lost on the rest of the audience. Benengeli's hat was, of course, an enormous turban and it was he who spoke to the knight and squire saying that he knew of both their past and future exploits and that this occasion was one of the latter. To be fair to Marco that paradox was almost worthy of our guest. He then announced my appearance as Dulcinea, represented as her real self by yet another wizard: in this kind of spectacular pantomime everything occurs by the agency of one mysterious power after another. I was being presented by the magic arts, no less, of the Celtic world's most renowned conjuror, Merlin. I'll say this, too, for Marco, he wasn't afraid of the obvious, he had a true theatrical imagination. Perhaps that is why he, our guest I mean (why can I never call him by his real name? I can't. I can't bring myself to write it down), why he never had any lasting success in the theatre? He is not a master of the obvious cleverly redecorated. For him everything must be qualified by contradictions which successively undermine the reader's certainty, even of what he's reading. It is a slowly dawning pleasure and mystery, quite the opposite of the quick duellings of drama. I mean, of course, it is a pleasure provided you do not find yourself portrayed as sinking in the amusing quagmire of his world.

Out of the wood we came accompanied by what he describes as soft and harmonious music. I was carried on a bier. He also writes that I was drawn by six grey mules but I wasn't. I was carried on the shoulders of twenty sweating villagers dressed in white. Beside me walked more, also in white but these wore the tall conical hoods of penitents, the kind the peg doll brought for me. They were bare-footed and chains trailed from their ankles. They carried long candles, Marco had even recruited two small boys to trim them. The bier was the one used in Holy Week for the effigy of the Blessed Virgin. I'll say one thing, your ladyship's a sight lighter than the Mother of God, one of the villagers told me during rehearsals. Jerónimo had presented the bier to the local church on our fifth wedding anniversary, hoping by this pious gift to quicken me into conceiving, if necessary immaculately, I suppose. It weighed many tons, the bier that is, not Jerónimo's hoped-for heir who never arrived. It was built of oak and superbly carved and gilded. I sat on an ornate throne surrounded by candles, I was even haloed by candles set in a wrought-iron hoop behind my head. I wore a dress of cloth of gold and a veil beneath a small crown. I have never felt more conspicuous. Beside me stood Merlin dressed completely in black with his cloak and hood masking his face.

We reached the pavilion and the music stopped. Everyone applauded. Merlin threw back his hood and cloak with a grandiloquent gesture and revealed himself as the skeletal figure of Death. Merlin was always a master of disguise. He was exactly like those capering skeletons we see before Easter, his legs and body being covered in tightly fitting black hosiery with the bones painted on in white. His face was made up as the skull, of course. Jerónimo and our guests laughed in delight and applauded again. Jerónimo, I noticed from behind my veil, was pretending to be frightened of this familiar apparition, falling back in his chair in mock horror. He was quite drunk by this time and anyway he loves to enter heartily into what he judges to be the spirit of things. In the theatre his distinctive guffaw has often embarrassed me, it is as if he imagines that only his over-audible approval can set the seal of success upon the occasion. Perhaps I'm too sensitive, it's a generous kind of patronage, really. Our guest laughed at his horseplay politely. Oh, his politeness, oh, his patience.

The skeleton coughed twice seeking undivided attention and Jerónimo subsided. He announced that he was not only Death but also Merlin who had resuscitated himself in this particular form by means of primordial techniques long forgotten by this modern world et cetera. Marco really overwrote Merlin's speech. And now it was his, Merlin cum Death's pleasure, to present the peerless Princess Dulcinea again by courtesy of his necromancy but, and this was our pageant's one dramatic moment, I was appearing only on parole as myself and if I were ever to achieve any permanency in this ideal form, rather than being what I really was, an ugly peasant girl with a hairy chest, then the knight's squire had to perform a penance. The penance was to whip himself three thousand three hundred times and on the last stroke I would be myself not as I had been until then but as I always ought to have been. Merlin never explained how I had happened to be mislaid in the first place but, of course, my author does, he can explain anything. A comical argument in short sharp lines followed between Merlin, the squire and the knight. Marco had an authoritative Greek name for this kind of chip-chop dialogue which I've forgotten but despite this it got a lot of laughs as the squire protested, refused, pretended to weep and the knight insisted. You can read all of this in, I nearly wrote the original, but the author took it all, virtually word for word, from Marco's pantomime.[1]

Now came my moment to perform. I drew aside the veil and everyone gasped. Marco had been right, it was a theatrical surprise, no one had expected me to be playing

[1] Cervantes's treatment of this masque may be found in *Don Quixote Part II*, Chapters 34 and 35. The instructions given by Merlin for the disenchantment of Dulcinea become a vital theme and the cause of a rift between the knight and squire which is never quite reconciled.

Dulcinea. But now suddenly our guest leaned forward, he looked at me with such direct, piercing attention that I panicked. There was a plummeting silence in which the words I'd learnt so easily weren't there, weren't anywhere, not in my head, not in my mouth, nowhere, they were gone. The pause seemed to me to last for at least half an hour before I heard Marco prompt me and I found I was speaking like someone from the dead, my voice didn't sound like mine or like that other when I speak from outside myself, no, it belonged to someone quite separate, a third person I had never met before who was telling the squire he must whip himself for my beleaguered beauty's sake. Of course he was persuaded eventually, huffing and puffing reluctantly, making amusing, down-to-earth provisos. There was more laughter (the kitchen boy stole the show and shortly after became rebellious while preparing vegetables), the melodious music began again, it was too hauntingly sweet for my taste but again Marco showed his instinct for touching the pulse of popular appreciation, the carts creaked away with Merlin and me behind them as the sun burst out with sudden redness from below the storm clouds so there was a sunset for the two heroes to ride away into which pleased Marco and the audience enormously. I did not take part in any of the other entertainments of that exceptional summer, to be two people sometimes is terrible enough, to be three is not to be borne.

We danced afterwards in the great hall and almost everyone complimented me on my performance. I asked almost everyone, but didn't you notice the awful silence before I spoke? What silence? You must have, I said, it seemed to me to go on for ever. There was a slight pause, we thought it most effective, most dramatic. It wasn't, it was like falling down a dried-up well. Really? Poor you. Surely you heard Marco prompt me? No. I couldn't understand it, I couldn't believe it, they must have noticed? I shan't act again, I said. Oh, but you must! You were wonderful. Smiles, endearments, kisses, it was most theatrical. And all the time he avoided me, me, his hostess, he who was always so polite talked to anyone but me. When I couldn't stand it any longer I marched up to him and said, well? And he said, you have taken the idea out of my head, Maribel. Have I? What idea? The whole play was Marco's idea and how could he have stolen your idea, you never tell anyone what you're writing? That's true, he said, and I haven't written it yet so it must be coincidence, why are you so fierce, Maribel? Because obviously you hated my performance, everyone else says I was wonderful. I'm sorry, I should have congratulated you at once, I know, but I couldn't. Why not? Because I needed time to think, to resolve the effect your appearance had upon me. You disturbed me profoundly, Maribel. And to think that I was pleased, that I interpreted that as my due! I smiled and he smiled. So you see, he said, I'm very glad the page's voice broke. Oh, you heard about that? Yes. I asked Marco how he had persuaded you to play Dulcinea and that's when he told me. Did I really live up to your invisible heroine? For an instant yes, but you're flesh and blood, Maribel, and so for the rest not quite, I'm afraid, but of course theatre is like that, and I can think of no one, no one who could have come so close, especially in the pause before you spoke, I thought for a moment you had forgotten your lines—I had, I explained, because you looked at me. Oh, it was my fault, was it? Yes, it was! Well, I'm glad because in that pause, which by the way was extraordinarily effective—I thought I was dying, I said, laughing now—it was in that pause that you looked, you were, for an instant, my sad, tired knight's visionary saviour. He's becoming tired now, Maribel, soon he will be doubly tired, after all, he wasn't a young man when he began, was he? Are you talking about your next book about him? Yes, I'm writing it here in the mornings. Is it going well? Better than ever. Don Quixote has just defeated another knight known as the Knight of the Mirrors. He is the complete hero now, he is successful in everything he does because he no longer quite believes in what he does. Oh, you haven't made him cynical, please don't make him cynical! No, I promise, I won't, but as the world honours him for what he was so he begins to doubt what he is. You mustn't tell me any more, I said, I don't want to hear any more, I want to be able to read it as a surprise. Of course, he said, I'm sorry, I've broken my own rule, haven't I?

At the end of his stay he gave me a book. When I opened it all the pages were blank. It is this book I'm using for this diary[1] but on one page, I didn't discover it till long after, I've reached it now, here it is, he had written a short verse:

> By hammering at his brain
> He made himself triumphal gates
> To a second lifetime,
> The desert of middle age
> Traversed by wrought-iron youth again,
> But at the last oh yet to be imagined
> His double tiredness
> At his double end.

That's all.

I next remember asking him what I had already wondered, did he mind our portraying his characters in a play? No, he didn't, he said. But in a way you were seeing yourself impersonated, weren't you, in the knight and squire? Possibly, but luckily nobody recognised me. Smile. Both actors were excellent but Rocinante and Sancho's donkey were even better, they were exactly as I imagined them. I think you do resent it really, I said. No, it was a generous compliment, my heroes are, I'm glad to say, public property now, published people, even if I haven't finished with them quite yet. Will you dance with me? I asked. Suddenly I wanted activity, exercise and the musicians were playing a volta in which you have to

[1] Cf. footnote to page 37.

bounce as if on springs and, oh, please, I said, dance with me. Please! Not me, Maribel, I'm too old. I must go to bed. And he did look old. For this kind of dance you need two hands as well as feet, he said and glanced at his left claw which I'd begun not to notice. Good night, Maribel, for one instant you achieved perfection, not many manage that.

We had given him a suite to himself with a private study and told the servants never to disturb him, to attend only if he called them. As a result the servants liked our guest extremely, he made no extra work. He had even refused a valet, preferring to dress himself. Jerónimo was shocked, no wonder the fellow always looks like a broody hen driven off her nest he said at least three times a week: when my husband employs a simile it has to earn its keep.

I danced with Count Braja whose particular sexual predilections preserve him as ever young, it seems. He voltas wonderfully, his arms feel as if woven from steel.

At four in the morning when the dawn chorus was beginning and I expect he was settling down to write, Jerónimo blundered into my room demanding conjugal satisfaction. I submitted, of course. I used to like the dawn chorus.

Juana has come in but she has no news. Where am I, here or there? Thin greasy soup, no bread. Here. I flung it out of the window.

I've slept, I who can never sleep in the afternoon. Am I becoming someone else of a more permanent kind than I am used to being? Someone who sleeps in the afternoon? They say you change as time passes, don't they? Well, he said so. But how completely does one change? Juana hasn't, nor has Jerónimo who could have easily got here by now, despite the snow. Perhaps he wasn't at the house when Dr Villanueva arrived? He could have gone away, I suppose, since his last letter? To Valladolid. My father's house, now Jerónimo's, might need attention, roofs do leak, walls can crack? Or, to Madrid now the Court's moved back to that model city full of frozen hopes, sun-cracked dreams. How I hate Madrid. Who knows, the King may have appointed Jerónimo as a special adviser for something, he's said to be always on the look-out for expert opinions? Jerónimo often hoped for such a call. Perhaps it has come at last? After all, men's careers continue to expand whatever the health of their wives and my husband has always had the habit of authority, he certainly looks expert even though his bluff brain has been eroded by winds of tobacco and waves of wine. No, I'm not here, I can't be here, won't be, here is too tenterhooked, too fearfully expectant.

He used to read in our library and I would go and read, too; what I could, so much was in Greek, and my Latin was wretched although I remember a rock in Virgil which marked the turning point for a boat race over bright blue waves with the oarsmen's hearts bursting with the effort to win while seabirds basked in the sun. He said he loved journals, everyday accounts by people doing extraordinary things such as explorers or soldiers. They were his favourite reading because they had so little colour, very few shadings of meaning, scarcely any of the subterfuges of the practised author. A good journal was like a good salad, he said, none of the goodness had been cooked out of the basic ingredients. Sometimes, of course, the writers, naive as authors but experienced as men, would attempt to colour, comment, generalise or philosophise, but it was easy to spot and skip those bits. Next to them he loved the patently absurd, the blatantly impossible, the novels of chivalry. Jerónimo had collected lots of these and I loved them, too. If only they had dried up Jerónimo's brain as they did that other knight's.

It was pleasant to talk to him in the library after an hour or two of companionable, page-turning silence. If you love these popular romances why do you make fun of them? Because I know them so well and am often tempted to write the same sort of thing. They contain everything except common sense whereas journals are all common sense. But they're so pompously written, even I can see that, and the heroes are always so good and the villains so bad? But you said you liked them, too, Maribel? Yes, but I'm not an expert like you and even I lose patience with them at times. I agree, so do I, but it is their wild absurdities which make them so cosily certain, you know where you are with such impossible people who aren't people at all, of course, but signs emblazoned with extravagantly virtuous or wicked devices while the world they inhabit expands, contracts, dissolves or resolves as the author wishes. You mean they are wooden people in a liquid world? I said. He laughed and praised me. I wanted his praise now, found more and more that I was trying to say things he would like. I'd begun to catch his tone. Words like you, Maribel, he said. I think it was that afternoon that we planned to write a play together for Marco to present. But the next minute I was angry because he began to tease me for criticising those lovely, improbable adventure stories, telling me I was more sophisticated than he was and I was laughing, too, more and more, but hating something inside myself and him and he commented on that saying it was all right because I was laughing when I wasn't really because there was an all-knowing side of him which really irritated me. I left in a rage.

That happened a lot later that summer. I used to remember that time as one golden glow with him as the sun warming me but it wasn't always like that at all. When he became too charmingly wise and knowledgeable, too wittily holier than thou I used to want to hurt him, to do something or say something which would force him to answer without thought, just once. To smoke out that animal which lurked behind his eyes, those brown eyes (were they his or that animal's?) which watched me so closely, so twinklingly or so blankly. I wanted to see what it was, was it in fact friendly, furry, cuddly? Old round tabby or watchful stoat? Both. I know now to my cost (why else am I here?) that authors contain their own opposites, always. I never did manage to hurt him, of course. He always deflected me, defeated me. So I resorted to tantrums naturally. Well, naturally for me.

But in between I was enchanted. He could tell so many stories, often with himself as the central character, he'd done so much apart from writing, travelled to so many places. He said he was, I didn't really believe him but it was true, a person to whom the most catastrophic things occurred. According to him, he had only to be invited aboard an admiral's flagship for it to sink in full view of the assembled fleet; he had only to stay at a remote country inn for it to burn down in the night; he couldn't help a passer-by hurt in a street brawl without the poor victim dying in his house so that he was accused of killing him.[1] I told him I hadn't realised he was such a liability to entertain but I must say that while he stayed with us several trivial yet inexplicable things did happen; they were amusing but for all that they had an edge of mystery. A stag's head fell for no reason from the wall as we walked up the stairs, two chairs broke under him (he wasn't a heavy or restless man) when he was with me, and I remembered his treading in the cowpat, not to mention a sudden fall on the lawn. We looked to see what could possibly have tripped him up and were forced to conclude against our better judgement that it had been a not especially upstanding buttercup. We both lay on the grass, laughing, laughing as if we were drunk which we weren't.

Juana liked him. He got on very well with her, imitating her Galician accent with such accuracy that she would beg him to stop, saying it made her homesick for hills and rain but she couldn't leave me. You're nobbut a wicked

---

[1] This incident is confirmed by many biographers of Cervantes. The first two occurrences are yet to be corroborated.

sprite, you munna split me in two, sir, she'd say. And he would stop, for her.

The peg doll has slipped a note under my door. It says: I continue to pray for you, madam.

I swim very well. It is one of the few things which makes me perfectly happy. There is a backwater in the woods about a mile from the house. Jerónimo had it cleared and deepened for me so I might bathe in privacy. It's a beautiful place surrounded by trees, lush grass and shrubs; a wild forest garden really full of butterflies and sometimes fallow deer appear to graze or drink as if we were not there. I used to swim every summer morning, usually with Juana who refused to undress but would paddle dutifully at my insistence then sit on the bank knitting or crocheting, sometimes with whoever of my ladies-in-waiting wanted to come. Those times were splashier, jollier. I still don't know why Jerónimo brought him there that morning. No, that isn't quite true, I think it was connected with his joking jealousy of our guest. That and some half-baked classical, school-boyish idea about nymphs surprised while bathing. A sort of Latin leer, dirty laugh, ho-ho encounter may have been in his mind. They did surprise us. Two booted men on horseback and us, five of us, without a stitch. I suppose it didn't matter really, only peasants mind about nudity, and I expect we made rather a pretty picture but I was furious, then worse, far worse, quite the worst I was while he was there. I still can't forgive Jerónimo. I was in the water with one of the other girls while the three on the bank snatched towels, clothes to cover themselves. Jerónimo was laughing loudly as he jumped off his horse and strode to the bank. Don't mind us, girls, he shouted or something equally stupid. We do mind, I called back. Go away, you promised me privacy here! I think our guest was embarrassed for the first time, Jerónimo had succeeded where I had failed to disconcert him. I think he wanted to ride away but couldn't out of deference to the Duke, my hearty

63

husband. It was the only time I saw him genuinely over-whelmed by rank. Even so he held back, did not dismount. Come on, Maribel, you can't stay in the water forever, shouted Jerónimo, come on out, girl. And you, you're Encarna, aren't you? Encarnación, the other girl who was with me, I was teaching her to swim, looked at me in dismay, she was only fifteen and very shy. The water was cold in the shade and Jerónimo had sprawled himself down on the bank just where we would have to get out. The other girls, safely but fetchingly draped by now, giggled and whispered together. They were start-ing to enjoy Jerónimo's joke. What would her ladyship do? They glanced from him to me. One of them, the boldest, María de los Angeles, who had learnt to enjoy my husband's tweaking finger and thumb and more, got up and offered him the wine and cakes we had brought with us. Still our guest held back. As she served Jerónimo she allowed her towel to slip. He was delighted, of course. Hey, Maribel, one of your girls knows how to entertain a gentleman! I began to shiver as much with rage as cold. Angeles turned away and I saw her approach our guest with lovely naked back and mincing buttocks. She was beautiful if rather large. I heard her say, do please dis-mount, sir, and share our picnic. Yes, come on, man, called Jerónimo with his mouth full of cake, the girls don't mind, my wife'll be out soon, she'll entertain us with her own hand. And *he* dismounted! I thought he'd ride away in disgust, but, no, he walked slowly to the bank. I couldn't believe it of him. But he didn't sit down on the bank, instead with careful deliberation he undressed completely, waded into the water and swam. Jerónimo roared with delight. I realise now that I didn't understand, that I quite misinterpreted this ultimate, delicate polite-ness of his. By undressing too, he redressed Jerónimo's crude discourtesy. But then, being in a panic of anger with my husband, I thought, very well, if this place is to be turned into a whorehouse, a sultan's bagnio, very well,

64

then at the least I'll be the madam or favourite concubine, very well, and I said to Encarnación, come along, it doesn't matter any more, and together we floundered to the bank and walked out of the cold water, goose-pimpled, into the sun. But poor Encarnación couldn't keep up with my bravado and with a shrill cry of purest shame ran away to hide in the bushes. Jerónimo laughed and laughed. I sat down clothed in water drops and accepted a glass of wine from Angeles with a trembling hand. Where's that fellow got to? said Jerónimo. He hadn't returned. We all looked, there was no sign of him. I ran along the bank, had he swum out to the river itself, its currents were dangerous? I glimpsed his head through the trees, yes, he was in the main stream, still swimming easily. Be careful, I called. He waved a hand to me and swam on. Come back, I shouted! Again he waved. I was desperate now. I ran back and said, why don't you help him, Jerónimo? He knows what he's doing, Maribel. But he could drown! Not he, he's the wisest man in the world, you told me so yourself, woman, what's the matter with you? I didn't reply, I dressed slowly as if Jerónimo no longer existed, as if Angeles, openly naked now, wasn't assiduously refilling his glass, as if Jerónimo's hand wasn't stretching forward to finger her breast, and began walking back alone, to the house. As I walked I found I was talking to myself, faster and faster, soon I was shouting and running and my voice was coming from the house as it came into view, I was at a high window screaming, I shall jump, you watch me jump, and there was Ramadan and I was leaning against him with my face buried in the dry tangle of his flopped-over hump crying I wish I were dead, he's dead so I wish I were! And I could hear the camel tearing uninterruptedly at the grass.

I don't know who found me there in the meadow but Dr Villanueva came the next day and I was given brandy while he bled me, opening the sutures in my legs for the first time. I learned later that this was the most modern treatment available and that it was the result of Dr Villanueva's own theory concerning the causes of hysteria in women. I didn't see anyone for six days except the doctor and Juana who insisted on nursing me. It was she who told me he had returned from the swim unharmed. On the seventh day Jerónimo appeared before me and he looked different, slack, shrunken, quiet. He was sorry, he said, it was all his fault, he said, he regretted his coarse joke, could I forgive him? I told him it was of no importance any more because the doctor had forbidden me to swim in future. Could I forgive him? he asked again. I didn't know if I could or not so I said yes and he smiled and straightened up a little. It seemed my forgiveness mattered to him but it didn't to me. I don't know why I did it, he said. I think I wanted to put a firework up that writer chap's backside, to see if there was any lead in his pencil, you and he were getting along so famously, was I jealous, do you think, Maribel? How can I know? I said, I don't know who you are. I'm your husband, Maribel. I meant apart from that, Jerónimo. Oh. He blushed and his eyes watered, I saw him brush at them with his hand. He said he was sorry again. Have you seen him? I said. Not much, he's shut himself up in his room, he's scribbling away up there, but how do *you* feel, Maribel? Calm, I said. The doctor's new treatment's working, you think? I don't think any more, Jerónimo. Oh. I'm simply very tired. Quite, I understand. And drained, Jerónimo. Well, that's all the bad blood gone, that's what Villanueva told me and we mustn't allow it to build up again, he says, all right, Maribel? I can't talk any more, Jerónimo, thank you for asking about me. Right, quite. I'll look in tomorrow, how's the appetite? I ate half a peach for breakfast. Good, that's the spirit. I won't ever do anything like that again, I promise, Maribel. Thank you, I said. Everybody's torn me off a strip, you should've heard Juana! He laughed hopefully. Did he? I said. No, he hasn't said a word, not a word, I meant everybody except him, funny chap, swims like a duck. Jerónimo kissed me on the forehead. My poor husband. He deserves a different wife, some big, placid creature with a broad sense of humour like his own, so they could just be two big babies tumbling on a blanket.

I recovered, although there were three more weeks of convalescence. Jerónimo would look in, as he called it, in the mornings, and eventually I began quite to enjoy his company. He would tell me all the doings of the house and estate, practical, solid, ordinary things which were nice to hear. And he, our author, would sit with me in the afternoons. I told him my life's history in daily instalments but I won't burden these pages with it, well, only those parts which he asked about.

The light's going, I must stop. Juana hasn't been allowed any more candles or wood for the fire so I must go to bed to keep warm. The chaplain, I assume, continues to pray for me while eating a hearty supper by the kitchen fire.

Saturday 5th February

I shall be allowed breakfast only when I have learnt by heart the marked passages in the books which the peg doll left with me on Thursday. Juana brought this message. The books have followed yesterday's soup into the court-yard below.

I would lie in bed by the window, he would sit beside me and I, of course, would ask him if I wasn't boring him? I told you, I like factual accounts best, he said. Did you like all your brothers and sisters? Oh, yes, they babied me, I was the youngest. So how were you able to bring so huge a fortune, dowry, when you married the Duke? When you had four brothers and two elder sisters? My father was very rich and I was the prettiest and his favourite, too. Besides that he had very unusual views on inheritance. My brothers hated him for them because he refused to promise them anything at all, nothing, not

67

even the eldest. He told them bluntly to make their own way in the world as he had done. He had begun with nothing, you see. You'll be telling me next he started as a blind man's boy! Well, nearly! It's all waiting for you in America, go and get it, he said to my brothers, but hurry, it won't last much longer, go before the English and French take it all. They went, except one, who became a priest and died of cholera in Barcelona. But the other three are all wealthy men now and revere my father's memory. They write in chorus that he gave them something more valuable than money, self-respect. You can tell from their letters that they have big, red, sun-burned faces. One grows sugar, the next tobacco and the third is a slave trader. And your sisters? Mercedes died when I was eight, the other one, Consuelo, married a French gentleman farmer, she has nine children already, she has one every year, she's very nice, she writes to me at Christmas and her letters always begin, well, I'm in pup again and then she advises me in detail of some new method she's heard of which will enable me to be as fertile as she is. One year I'm told to give Jerónimo a piece of jasper on a chain to wear, the next that powdered bull's horn is the thing for me to eat when the moon is waxing. I tend to think of her as more a peapod than a person. He smiled. So you were the only one to marry into the nobility? No, my eldest brother Francisco Jesús has an Indian princess for a common-law wife. He laughed. Don't Indian princesses count? I asked. Oh, yes, I'm sure they do, he said.

I'm ravenous. I do hope Juana succeeds in stealing something from the kitchen, bread, sausage, a carrot, anything.

My father spoilt me completely. I could have anything I wanted, even education. This really angered my mother, and me sometimes, when I found I didn't like my tutor after all. Why teach a girl? she'd shout at my father, you'll only ruin her looks! What were you taught, Maribel?

Reading and writing, music, geometry, astrology, Latin which I hated although Greek was worse, I rebelled violently over Greek. Oh, and riding and dancing, my mother didn't mind about those, she could see the marriage value in them, and swimming. I blushed. That had slipped out without thinking. Well, you know all about that, I said. Yes, he said, your husband put us both in an unexpected position. But we called his bluff, didn't we, Maribel? I don't know, I said, it led to another illness, didn't it, quite the worst I've ever known? No, the Duke's immodest joke did that. You blame my husband? Absolutely, he deceived both you and me, Maribel. He didn't tell you before that that was where we bathed? No, that was why I swam, too, so you and I could both be equal in nakedness in front of him. I see, I said, but Jerónimo's ashamed now. I daresay he is. Quite contrite. Good. You sound very hard? Yes. Yet you continue to accept his hospitality? Only until you are well again, Maribel. I laughed, oh, in that case I shall stay ill so you can't go. But now you must forgive Jerónimo just as I have. Please. And, you know, in a way it's turned out for the best because now I feel I can tell you anything, show you anything, such as what this doctor is doing to me. And trustingly, like a child, I pulled up my gown and showed him. He winced. And remembered.

Where is Juana? My tummy keeps talking louder than my head.

Did you know that Jerónimo's got three children? He's very proud of them, they're all boys, they would be, wouldn't they? One by a lady-in-waiting, another by a chambermaid, I dismissed them, of course, and the third, the eldest, by a fat girl in Flanders. That one's nearly ten now, he's a page with the Marquis of Villel, he's the spitting image of Jerónimo, apparently. What's his name? he asked. Rodrigo. I may have met him. How? Do you know the Marquis of Villel? Yes, he wrote to me after the publication of my book and invited me to stay with him.

I spent several days at one of his country houses near Teruel. It was a very green place and a very quiet, gracious house. I envied the Marquis. Greener, quieter, more gracious than here? Much, he said, but his smile said he was teasing me. Do you make a habit of holidaying in noble houses? I used to, he said, I made a lot of friends when I was a tax collector. I couldn't believe him, you a tax collector? I said, you? And do tax collectors actually make friends? He laughed. Incompetent ones do, yes. It was a difficult job and in the end I went to prison. You've been to prison? Twice. Once in Algiers for ransom and once in Seville for embezzlement. At least I was charged with embezzlement but it was really a mixture of bad bookkeeping and greed on the part of a judge. How long were you in prison? Seven months. I shall always remember the judge, he was the smallest complete man I have ever seen. He was a perfect manikin, very handsome with jet-black eyes, a diminutive dandy, everything about him was in proportion except his desire for money. But he wasn't content with simply sentencing me to jail, oh no, he felt obliged to deliver a homily as well. He had the most beautiful speaking voice. He gave me and the world, well, the seven people in the public gallery, it wasn't a sensational case, you understand, just a question of accounts not balancing correctly and who had pocketed the deficit? He gave us the dulcet benefit of his reflections upon my character which he found to be dishonourable. He was a popular judge, well known for his inclination to lighten a sentence or even find in favour, whatever the evidence, provided the accused could reinforce his defence with what is known in the legal profession as a substantial *quid pro quo* and in the back streets as an offer no gentleman can refuse. I couldn't afford what he called my bail which he found incomprehensible because since he insisted that all my evidence was false it followed that I must have salted my gains away somewhere and was therefore wilfully, reprehensibly withholding them from

70

their rightful place inside his pocket. Consequently I had to face the full force of his propriety. We laughed. I said, you liked telling me that, didn't you? Yes, it's easy to tell now, but it was less easy to endure at the time. Did you mind being in prison? It was a mixed blessing.[1] I think I would kill myself if I were sent to prison! Didn't you meet the most dreadful people, murderers, thieves? No, most were inside for the same offence as myself, poverty. But not all, surely? No, but even they, having committed their violent crimes, had since reverted to their former selves, I met very few monsters of inhumanity. Can you really forgive everyone, really? Oh, no, not quite everyone. I cannot forgive my judge, for instance. Because he was a hypocrite, do you mean? No, not because of that, most of us are hypocritical, Maribel, in some corner of ourselves. Hypocrisy is often a small force for good, however distasteful it may seem, because when we occasionally pretend to be better than we really are, we are at least acknowledging that there exist virtues which ought to be respected and perhaps our pretence may serve to prevent us from being worse than we otherwise would be. One might call hypocrisy a mildly elevating vice when pettily indulged. Besides, people often begin by pretending to be good for perfectly ignoble reasons and then, despite themselves, almost become so. Life lasts a long time whatever the priests say and many of us simply get too tired to be bad. We grow into our disguises. But not everybody! Your theory doesn't fit everyone, it can't. No, I wish it could, Maribel, I agree. Then what is it you don't forgive your judge for? For enjoying his power over me, a stranger to him. He took pleasure in hurting me.

Juana's come back at last! She's stolen a cold potato omelette meant for the peg doll!

---

[1] This is the only reference in the diary to the disputed whereabouts of the conception of *Don Quixote*. It is too ambiguous, however, to confirm Cervantes's own ambiguity, since all he says in the preface to *Part I* is that his idea is 'very much like one engendered in prison'.

It was wonderful, like a thick yellow plate, never has anything tasted so good. If Jerónimo were to come now I could answer him. Eating has even made my hands warm again.

There was another person he couldn't forgive just as I can't forgive him. Our chaplain. I don't mean the peg doll but his predecessor, Father Gattinara. After the first evening they never even said good morning to each other. It was our first dinner together and Jerónimo and I were excited and flattered that he had arrived at last. We'd invited him a whole year before and he'd accepted but kept changing the date for various reasons, so many people less provincial than us wanted to entertain Spain's newest great author. In the end we didn't receive his last letter saying he was coming so his arrival was quite unexpected. I had given up all hope. So we were just family at that first dinner: Jerónimo, me, Jerónimo's maiden aunt, Carlota, Father Gattinara and him, our guest. Even so my husband insisted we dine in the great hall which I thought was a mistake because we were so few in that great echoing cavern. All the talk was about the book, of course, which I loved then, I couldn't talk about it enough, I'd read it four times. It's difficult at this distance to convey the excitement it created, not only in me and Jerónimo, but in everyone else. It was so new, so different, so shining, no, I can't adequately recall the sensations we felt at that time. I remember thinking, hoping that our guest was pleased to find we weren't entirely rustic gentlefolk although our social horizons were less wide than the valley of the Ebro's real ones. He and I seemed to take to each other at once, it was as if I had known him for years, I seemed able to make him laugh and he seemed able to make me more amusing, cleverer than I was, but I've said this before. The only sour aspect at dinner was the chaplain. He was thoroughly put out by our visitor. He grunted and glowered as the conversation blossomed. I knew why. Father Gattinara was used to leading the talk at our often rather silent family meals. And even when we entertained he would dominate a corner of the table considering himself a man of broad learning which was true and of wit which was also true except that his jokes took such a long time to be born. Waiting for one of them was rather like waiting for the second coming, you knew it had to arrive eventually but when, when? He was a master of parentheses which he established like forts along the frontier of his main argument to withstand interruption. The subjects closest to his heart were the degeneracy of the King, the perniciousness of Luther, the training of hunting dogs and his vendetta against what he called the new scientists by whom he meant Galileo, that presumptuous, unwashed pisspot as he put it. Father Gattinara prided himself on sudden franknesses of expression after interminable circumlocutions. But that evening it was we who talked and thanks to our guest our conversation seemed to be a lovely soap bubble floating higher and higher until plurp, Father Gattinara had banged, was still banging the handle of his knife on the table. If I may speak, he said, his voice pontifical with the wine he'd drunk during his enforced silence, if I may possibly speak, and the prow of his jowled face wallowed at us like that of a fishing smack in a swell, if I may be permitted to introduce a note of what one might well call healthful scepticism, and he smiled from side to side which was always a bad sign, or indeed downright disbelief, ha, ha, ha, if he laughed within the fabric of his subordinate clauses it was time to shut off what remained of your mind, then I should like to seize this opportunity to say—By all means, father, said Jerónimo, interrupting bravely, but please mind my cutlery, you'll split the handle. Vanity, sir, vanity, snorted the chaplain. Jerónimo made a face and I laughed but luckily managed to sneeze it away. Do speak, father, your introduction has left us all agog. Jerónimo was quick and easy that night, quite his best. And, horror, he got up,

73

Gattinara actually rose from his chair. I couldn't help myself. I said, you don't really need to stand, father, we aren't a synod of bishops, are we? Would you were, your ladyship, would you were, because then I might hope that what I have to say would be acted upon to the general benefit of mankind. But it's just us, father, said Jerónimo. In that you are deceived, sir, we have a guest, and his eyes turned to him, a guest whom I shall liken to that famous engine or equine quadruped which the deluded of Troy dragged into their beleaguered city at night only to bewail their fate by dawn. Oh, Lord, I thought as I glanced at our guest, how would he, how could he, respond to such insulting verbosity? He sat very still, then shut his eyes, pinching the corners between finger and thumb, then opened them again and smiled as if he had warded off a headache. Oh, do sit down, father! Jerónimo was close to explosion. I prefer to stand, indeed I will not sit longer in this person's presence, sir. This was too much. Jerónimo jumped to his feet. In that case, Gattinara, we must leave you. Come along, Maribel, Aunt. My dear sir, I can only apologise for our chaplain's rudeness, if it weren't for his cloth I should take pleasure in challenging him on your behalf, ours is a small world in which he has grown fat, I'm afraid. But he remained seated. He said, no, please, I should like to hear what your chaplain has to say, his vocation guarantees his compassion and his age his wisdom, possibly. He said it so mildly, so gently that Jerónimo had to sit down again. Very well, sir, he said, as you wish. Do go on, father, at our guest's request. The chaplain took breath, I heard it wheeze in his chest, and he began. I was reminded of a carpenter hammering down floorboards.

I understand you consider yourself an author, sir, upon the evidence of single popular novel? That you imagine you have secured yourself a place upon Parnassus? And this book I propose to question is a work of fiction, is it not? A work which purports to satirise other fictions no

less undistinguished than itself? You present for our entertainment, I have it upon reliable report, a foolish country
nobleman of advanced years who behaves as if the age
of chivalry were not dead and who, out of his insanity,
engineers farcical exploits for himself in which he imagines
windmills to be giants, flocks of sheep to be armies—our
guest held up his hand, our chaplain overrode him—I
shall allow you time to reply presently, sir. Now allow
me to ask you a question and I suggest you weigh your
answer well. Ponderous poked-neck pause. You've already
asked me four and a half and I can't know if your next
is worth a reply until you ask it, so please don't pause for
me, I can follow your argument without pauses. Jerónimo
laughed, Gattinara's jowls wobbled, growing purpler. You
regard yourself as a man of wit, sir? Is that your next
question? And still he smiled, it was my first experience
of his deadly patience. No, sir, it is not! snorted Gattinara.
My question is this: in what particular does your work,
which has reputedly bemused the entire nation, not to
mention your noble hosts who have honoured you, in my
view undeservedly, with their bread and board, in what
particular or undeniable instance does your so-called book
differ from the trash it sets out to ridicule and furthermore
what is the precise nature of its superiority and what
evidence have you that its effect upon the moral health
of its readers is not as deplorable as the deleterious influence of its progenitors since all fiction is in my view,
and in that of others even more qualified to judge than
myself, sir, pernicious in that it inveigles our superiors from
their duties and our inferiors, by which I mean the
ignorant and simple-minded, from their lowly tasks because
such persons are unable to distinguish a work of fiction
from a work of truth and are thus laid open to the
sensational and corrupt ideas of modern authors such as
yourself, sir, who have no worthier ambition than the
amassing of money to which I would place the addendum,
corollary, appendix that the subject matter of your scurrilous

75

fiction is self-evidently subversive, irresponsible, nay vicious, since it presents the nobility to the common run of people as a laughing stock thus striking at the very fabric of our society, indeed, sir, I am astonished and appalled that you have not been arraigned for treason although that may yet, with God's help, occur. I trust it may.

It is dark. I'm tired. I must leave his answer until tomorrow. I've asked Juana to share my bed tonight to keep me warm. I hope I can sleep. I tell myself not to think about the future but the only sure way left to me is this diary. When I write in this book tomorrow disappears, I become entirely yesterday.

Sunday 6th February

Our guest said (he did not get up, he left standing up to Father Gattinara), he said, have you read my book? Jerónimo laughed aloud. Certainly not, sir! I see, he said. But why didn't he say the obvious next thing? How dare you condemn what you haven't read? He was new to me then, of course. Instead he let that question hover not quite asked over everything that followed. Your critique was comprehensive, father, its preamble contained, as far as I could count, five and a half rhetorical questions, then three real ones inside the main discourse, then none at all in what I can only describe as a rabble-rousing appeal for me to be garrotted. Only there is no rabble here. I must admit I find it difficult to answer you in any way, either rhetorically which is very much your style, it seems, or more plainly which is mine, I hope. Your mind looks closed to me. I know very little about you, of course, and I'm not sure you know very much about me, although you claim to. We may well be strangers to each other. I should guess that you are an impassioned idealist like myself, except your ideals are different from mine. Still, I'll try to answer you. Please don't expect me to be as convinced as yourself, like Sancho Panza I doubt everything and believe everything, oh, I'm sorry, you haven't read my work, have you? Nor seen my plays? Nor read my published verses? Your first real question first, yes, there is a difference between my novel and those others, mine takes place in the real world, they do not. Your second, how is it superior to them, is also simply answered, it is funnier. Your third, about its effect on the reader being as bad as those other popular books, I cannot answer. Ha! trumpeted the chaplain, scenting triumph. I can't answer it because I've never been able to find any reliable way of measuring a decay of moral health in someone through what he reads. Had you read my book you might be able to say that while my hero suffers a decay of mental health his moral health is actually improved by what he reads, so much so that, after a lifetime of doing nothing at all, he sets out nobly but absurdly to assuage the world's sorrows. He may be as much of a fool as his author but his intentions are of the best Your imputation that I wrote Don Quixote's history solely for money I attribute to your ignorance and I reject it with the contempt I have for all bigoted philosophers who project their own deficiencies of understanding on to the world in the disguise of righteous indignation. Such people remind me of lunatic cartographers mapping worlds they have not measured. I could say more but I won't, your style is too infectious, father, and I shouldn't wish to catch a disease which makes the sufferer sacrifice truth to noise. Finally, as to which one of us is right, I leave to my hosts, who *have* read my book, to decide, good night.

And he got up and left the hall as quietly as he had spoken. Jerónimo followed him at once and Aunt Carlota who had said very little all evening suddenly spoke. What a nice man, she said, if he wasn't a writer I'd call him a gentleman.

The next morning Father Gattinara formally requested a month's leave of absence to visit his aged mother in

Cuenca. Jerónimo granted it. The house became much lighter.

Oh, no! The peg doll has appeared in the courtyard. He's gone to the main gate. I can see him from here as I write. There's something expectant, almost tiptoe about him as he peers through the gates. I've had a disgusting thought, a jolt! I shouldn't be writing these memories of that summer, he's lulled me into inactivity when I ought to be thinking how to escape. Could I? Juana would come with me, I know she would. But where would we go? We couldn't walk and we haven't got horses. The peg doll's? Chica? But the stables are in the courtyard and there's no way out of the courtyard except by the gates which are always locked. Lead Chica, she's a docile mare, through the house itself and out the back way? One could. No, absurd. Clip clop on the flagstones through the hall, dining room to the left, chapel to the right, under the main stairs and down the passage to the kitchens? Muffle her hooves? No, Maribel, you're not a conspirator, you can't do incredible things as if they were normal, no. And yet? Oh, he's turned away from the gates, he's going across to the stables, Chica's put her head out, I see why, he's produced a carrot from his cassock and she's chewing it. He's patting her nose and she doesn't mind his touch. Oh, God, he's looked up at my window!

I left the table at once. Did he glimpse me as I turned away from the soft lance of his gaze? Like cuckoo spit on a green shoot? Oh. He's come back in again now, he's somewhere below me. He ought to take more care of Chica, she'll be getting out of condition, she's had no exercise for four days now and she has a tendency to plumpness anyway.

An hour later and there's a pale gleam of sunlight on this page. But I can't return to my house by the river either in thought or deed. Having imagined the possibility of escape I can't think of anything else today.

But where, where could I go? I've no money. All I've
got are three rings I was wearing when Jerónimo brought
me here, he must come tomorrow, oh, God! I'm in a
mesh, caught like a bird in a net, entangled in improbable
possibilities. Speculation, my heart's bursting with speculation. When it's dark I'm going to hide this diary in the
chimney, there's a little ledge, I've looked. It will be quite
safe, we've used up all the firewood. Oh, I want to get
back to where I was, but I can't. Hide it, hide this book,
because if they come they'll take it, confiscate it, I know
they will, and if they do that—hide it!

Tuesday 8th February

Jerónimo came yesterday and left yesterday. He arrived
with what I can only describe as a small army. Twelve
men at arms! What did he expect me to do? And Dr
Villanueva. He's ordered a more regular but still restricted
diet. I can't eat anything. I've been forcibly bled and
officially scourged. My husband supervised both operations
with implacable courage and tears pouring down his
cheeks. When I am fully recovered from his corrections the
chaplain (I shan't refer to him as the peg doll again, that
would be disrespectful) and six of the soldiers are to escort
me to the convent. I can't write more today.

Wednesday 9th February

I'm shaky but a little better. I've told Juana to say I'm
still too weak to travel but we have to be careful because
they've removed the lock from the door so my room may
be entered at any time by those who care for me. The
chaplain comes and prays for me at my prayer stool seven
times a day. He is indefatigable in his new devotions for
me. There is a soldier on guard in the corridor all day
and all night. The courtyard clock has been repaired or
rewound, I don't know which. Jerónimo's visit has

prompted a kind of phosphorescent life in this box. I still dream of escape but in a faraway sort of way. Any will I had recovered before my husband came has quite gone.

I realise now I have been far too generous to Jerónimo. Remembering him as he was eight years ago and not seeing him for weeks had made me, I can't say understanding, but I had begun to think how difficult it must have been for him to be married to me. Then, Monday came at last, crash, a storm of fire and blood. Yes, fire, they lit a fire, the flames leapt up the chimney and this book was there where I'd hidden it! I screamed, they thought I was mad, of course, but I wasn't, I was just fearful for my diary, the only thing I have which is entirely mine. But it survived, with me. After they'd gone I crawled to the chimney, kicked the logs aside, I didn't care if I was burnt. It was hot, covered in soot but unharmed, the flames had leapt past the ledge. I hugged it to me and thanked God, thanked God. I still do.

Do I exaggerate about Jerónimo? He was only performing as his conscience dictated and his advisers advised. He could have killed me, he'd been drinking spirits from a flask all the way up. He drank more while he was with me. He wore a helmet, a breastplate and a sword. I begged to speak to him by himself, asked him to remove his helmet, I can't talk to a public fire bucket, I told him, but his red-eyed determination knew no bounds, could hear nothing I said, why does nobody listen to me? They never have, they never do, except him, my author. Was that why I loved him? And then Jerónimo's crocodile tears. Were they? I don't suppose even he knew as he engineered the re-establishment of his authority over me, had me stripped in front of—no, I can't describe the horror of my double correction, medical and spiritual, I thought I could, but I can't, it would foul the page. I wish *he* could have seen it though.

I did write to him just before Christmas, wrote for the very last time saying how could you, you've made me totally recognisable, how could you be so kind to me in person, so vile in ink? If he replied I didn't receive his letter. Perhaps because two weeks later I was imprisoned here or was it because I signed my letter the Duchess whose Title is Wellknown?[1] He could have put it aside with all the other cranky letters famous authors receive. No reply, no explanation, no apology. And all the while, all through that ruined Christmas, with the house awash with Jerónimo's family, guests, music, my husband was hissing in public at me or shouting in private that there wasn't any offence in the book at all. I've nearly finished it now, I sat up all night last night reading it just to be sure, please be sensible, Maribel, everyone's wondering what's the matter with you, he's only done what every author does, only changed what happened while he stayed with us into a story, for God's sake! It isn't serious, it isn't a serious book, it's a novel, for Heaven's sake! Of course I recognise various things, incidents, of course. Those pageants we put on for him, but even there he's made everything much larger than life and teased it out so that it suits his story not ours, not us, Maribel. I fetched the book then, opened it at the very page, and said, and that? Read that! Read it again, Jerónimo!

I shall record it here, it's engraved on my heart: "What ails my lady the Duchess? asked Don Quixote. Do you mark, sir, said the waiting-woman, the beauty of my lady? That smoothness of her face that is like a polished sword, those two cheeks of milk and vermilion, in one of which she has the sun, in the other the moon? And that state with which she moves, trampling and despising the ground as if she dispensed health wherever she goes? Know, sir, that first she may thank God for it, and next two issues that she has in both her legs, at which all the ill-humour is let out, of which the physicians say she is full. Holy Mary, said Don Quixote, is it possible that my lady the

---

[1] María Isabel is misquoting ironically Cervantes's own words: the Duchess whose Title is Unknown.

Duchess has such outlets?"

That is what my husband read, what anyone can read, and yet all he said was, you must have told him yourself? Did you? I know I didn't because I hardly spoke to him after your treatment began, which I considered confidential, anyway. But he was constantly enjoying your company and, I daresay, your girlish confidences, so I imagine you've brought it on yourself, Maribel, don't you? I agree it is a quite unnecessary detail, a slip of the pen which I should have thought he'd have had the good taste to cross out. But what does it matter? It's old history, water under bridges, woman, no one else knew, did they? Juana did. She's loyal, you always say. Besides you haven't been bled for three years at least now, have you? You're better, or rather you were until this damned book appeared, and to think I thought it would give you pleasure! Mind you, if you don't pull yourself together soon I shall have to ask Dr Villanueva to start again. Oh, no, no, Jerónimo, please. Oh, yes, I shall. You've hardly been a gracious hostess this Christmas, have you? Mother said to me yesterday, María Isabel may have brought you money, dear, but precious little else, she doesn't seem like a wife at all. I had to laugh that off, Maribel. It wasn't easy, my mother's a very perceptive woman. So my advice is you're to forget this wretched book, forget it, it isn't as good as the first one anyway, I didn't laugh nearly so much, if you ask me the author's written himself out, as they say.

Even I could see that that wasn't true. The sequel was far better, deeper and darker, which was why it hurt me to be seen as part of it, to be shown as the guiding spirit, the smiling torturer of his heroes whom the reader has learnt to love so much. Me, a beautiful shell concealing heart-constricting poison, an alabaster Diana with envenomed arrows. Me, pretending to be so charming to them yet meanwhile arranging their next humiliation, bewildering them in public, assaulting them in private, hoodwinking them again and again and again. And my house,

82

my lovely house, a torture chamber. It wasn't an unnecessary detail at all, it was essential to his purpose in
fixing me in place and time, like a butterfly pinned to a
piece of card. He knew what he was doing, writing. He
says he's the finest author in the world at the end of his
book and it isn't a joke or bravado, it is true and he
knows his reader knows it.

On New Year's Eve I refused to come down to dinner.
Jerónimo called the doctor as he had promised he would.

Tuesday 22nd February[1]

I'm allowed to wear shoes because I'm not even a novice
yet. But my head has been shaved, it's the rule here. The
Mother Superior is very kind. The habit I wear is quite
warm sackcloth. I think I must already be rather a favourite
in this sisterhood, at least with the younger nuns because
one of them lent me her secret mirror for a moment, it
was just a little broken bit no bigger than a key ring.
Without hair I look like a young turnip.

I'm going to leave soon. I tell them all that at least
three times a day so they won't believe me. Juana is
allowed to visit but not to live here. She is staying a
mile away with a farmer and his family, she says they let
her work for her keep, but what work is there on a
mountain farm in this winter weather? At least I no longer
see the chaplain.

We're very high up here but also very low down because
the convent is in a ravine which is the dead end of a
valley where the pine trees grow immensely tall towards
a jagged strip of purest blue between the peaks. It has been
very cold and sunny since I was brought here. I think
there may be clouds lower down but I don't know. My
days are divided by little bells which tell me to do things
like wash, pray, eat, sleep, pray, sleep, pray. They've
allowed me to keep this diary but only after I made a

[1] This gap of thirteen days becomes self-explanatory.

tremendous fuss. There are six other distressed gentle-women here, all much older than me but equally unwanted by their families, and I know now that each of us has been allowed to keep a small memento. One, she must be sixty at least, has a doll, another an old towel which is filthy, she will never let it be washed, when she hugs it to her she can talk quite sensibly, and there's another one, very tall and grand-looking who wears a feathered hat which looks very strange on top of a coif. We all have one thing like that which means a lot to us but doesn't really matter. The Mother Superior is very understanding, she reminds me of one of those coiled buns like puffy plates on sale on public holidays. She's very strict with her girls as she calls the nuns but more lenient with her ladies as she calls us. I suppose that's because our families are paying the convent so much to keep us here. She does insist that we write home regularly to say how nice it is, which it is, really. Jerónimo does not answer my letters, but I expect he is very busy. Before I was in a stone box, now it's more like a stone stomach you can walk quietly about in. I walk a lot, up and down the corridors, into the chapel, into the cloisters, into the refectory, into the kitchens even. I can walk everywhere except outside. Sometimes I'm obeying the bells, of course, but other times I'm not.

I don't sleep very much, again because the little bells keep calling us to jump out and pray. I've made up my own prayer, it's quite short, it says, please help me understand everything as he does. I'm always saying it. The other reason I don't sleep is the other ladies, we're all in the same dormitory and there's a little high place in the wall where a nun sits watching us all night. The other ladies talk a lot either because they're awake or asleep. It doesn't seem to make much difference, they talk. Sometimes you can understand them, sometimes you can't. The lady with the doll barks a lot, there's another who insists, sleeping and waking, that she's as light as air, she's made rather a friend of me, she says, I can see you down there, Maribel, I'm hovering over you, look. I think I did see her fly once but I expect it was a dream.

There's the bell for compline.

Wednesday 23rd February

I'm absolutely furious! Juana is paying that farmer out of her own savings while Jerónimo rolls in my money! If only my father were alive or my brothers weren't so far away! Well, it's another reason for leaving. I will not have Juana put to expense on my account. We think it may be easier to escape from here than from the hunting box.

We did try. We both dressed as warmly as we could and at two o'clock one morning, there was no moon, we crept out past the sleeping guard in the corridor. We felt very expert, we were childish really. We'd dared the guard who was little more than a boy, seventeen at most, to drink some brandy Juana had stolen from the kitchen. One glass followed another as we teased him, telling him soldiers drank brandy like water, didn't they? Soon he was sleeping like a cherub on the chair we'd insisted on giving him. How we congratulated ourselves.

Down the stairs, feeling our way across the pitch-black hall, trying not to giggle at our success so far, out into the sudden starlit cold of the courtyard, and across to the stables. There was nothing we could do about our footprints in the snow. Chica behaved beautifully. She let us harness her without a sound, let us muffle her hooves with pieces of sacking we found in her stall. Not a snort, not a whinny, Juana talked to her all the time in Galician. Then we led her back across the courtyard to the front door, up the four broad steps, we had to be very patient with her there, she jibbed twice at the steps before rushing them and coming to a rigid halt in the hall. But we had still made no real sound except our whispers to the mare, that's right, up we go, what a clever girl, good girl, shush!

85

Under the stairs into the passage which leads to the kitchens, Juana tiptoeing ahead. Slowly she opened the door at the end of the passage. The game larder, its unseen shelves and hooks still smelling of putrefaction. The door creaked a little, Chica snorted in alarm, but my hand on her nose quietened her. The next door, the one to the main kitchen, was outlined by light opposite us. The cook had left the kitchen fire in, it seemed. We crept across, lifted the latch and there was the chaplain reading by the bright fire. I don't know who was more startled as he looked up, yes, I do, Chica, who reared back, hitting her head on the lintel. She whinnied in terror, a piercing, unearthly sound which quite drowned the chaplain's exclamations. She tried to back into the larder, tried to turn, trod on Juana's foot. The chaplain got up, whereupon Chica charged headlong into the kitchen. We ran with her, there was a table between the three of us and the chaplain who'd starting shouting for the guards. Chica was in a sweat now, neighing and plunging and bucking as we tried to drag her through. Hams and sausages fell from the ceiling, the grindstone went flying, pots and pans were swept by her tail to the floor. We were all shouting at once but then we heard the clatter of boots on the stairs above, pounding closer, closer. Juana and I ran, we let go of Chica and ran, out through the sculleries, out of the back door, across the yard, past the barn and the dairy, the place was a midden under the snow, we were up to our knees. I fell, Juana pulled me out, but I was crying with rage, shouting, how stupid, how very stupid, how stupid!

They caught us, of course. Four soldiers in boots but no trousers. They marched us back to the kitchen as if our attempt to escape had been serious. The chaplain was standing holding Chica's bridle and patting her nose as if quietening a horse in a kitchen was the most usual thing in the world. We were ordered to stand by the fire while Chica was handed over to one of our guards who led her out to the barn. But as she left she defecated neatly on to the kitchen floor; the sweet wholesome country smell filled the room and made me smile. Chica had demonstrated her pedigree. The chaplain felt obliged to fulminate at us as the soldiers looked on, proudly sheepish, I interrupted him, low comedy needs no epilogue, chaplain, good night.

The next day I was escorted to this sisterhood. And two days later I was given a short letter from Jerónimo, his last. It said, as far as I can remember, I tore it up, smaller and smaller until my fingers ached, it said, I shall not write to you again, madam, to me you are dead. Meanwhile I am exploring vigorously the legal and ecclesiastical requirements for the annulment of our marriage, from my hand, et cetera. Meanwhile? Meanwhile what? Meanwhile?

But the astonishing thing is, despite all these recent disasters I feel happier, more optimistic than I have for years. I feel graceful and controlled. Perhaps it's the mountain air? I don't know.

Thursday 24th February

I feel as serene today as I did yesterday, as serene as I felt I did towards the end of his visit when we were writing our play together, the play with the magic horse with the lever in his forehead.

The story we concocted was a pretext for the spectacle of this carpentered animal actually flying overhead, above the audience, well, sliding on ropes and pulleys which we couldn't conceal from the spectators. Even so they all applauded enthusiastically, apprehensively. We sent his two heroes on a mission to relieve a countess and her ladies-in-waiting of their beards. They were, of course, under the spell of a malevolent giant because the countess had been governess to a princess who had fallen inappropriately in love with a young gentleman of lower birth than herself. The doting countess had helped the lovers to meet and when the princess found herself pregnant she had arranged a secret marriage for them. On hearing of this the princess's mother, Queen Magancia (fancy my remembering her name! It must be the clear air here) died of shock, heartbreak and sheer snobbery. Her sudden death brought her first cousin, the giant who also happened to be a wizard, flying to her grave on his wooden horse and 'by his magic arts' he turned the young married couple into a group statue to ornament the tomb. The princess was turned into a brass monkey (his idea) and the youth into a crocodile made of an unknown metal (my idea). The giant then gazed with malignant eye upon the countess and her ladies who had been responsible for the entire social catastrophe. His first thought was to kill them but he commuted the sentence into what the countess called a living death by magicking beards on to their chins instead. After that he posted a notice on the tomb to the effect that all the protagonists would remain as they were until the world-famous Don Quixote arrived in person to challenge him to combat. You can tell how happy we were by the badness of the story but he said that was only the background plot. It took us several afternoons to work it out but I expect his allowing me to help was a hindrance. Without me he could probably have dashed it off in quarter of an hour or less. When I say we wrote it together I mean we discussed it in detail and then he wrote it out and I would comment solemnly upon it and sometimes he'd change it to please me. I became happier and happier. His presence every afternoon, his patience, I realise now how tedious it must have been for him to collaborate with such an amateur, and his enthusiasm for the projected pantomime made me feel I was a person again. He and Marco, who loved all the mechanics required for the play, could have organised it all so easily between themselves. But never once did he make me feel unwanted or superfluous and during one of these discussions I suddenly said, I love you, I hadn't expected to say it, it was said before I realised what I was saying, I wasn't embarrassed, nor was he,

I think, but then I suspect he was used to being loved. He didn't laugh, thank God. He said, as if I really deserved an answer, I'm three times your age, Maribel. I know that, I said and now I was embarrassed. Well, knowing that you will know that that difference matters, apart from many other things, and if I were to explain it would irritate you a great deal because I would be bound to sound so, so paternal, Maribel. I don't think of you as three times my age, you don't look sixty and most of the time you seem younger than Jerónimo. That's because your husband has responsibilities. Don't you? He sighed. No, he said, authors don't, well, not any the world recognises. Also I've learnt to forgive myself, that makes anyone seem younger. What do you mean? When I was neither young nor old, in what people call the prime of life, I always assumed I could do better than I did at everything. I was in a perpetual impatience with myself, my aspirations flew ahead of my abilities, like a covey of partridges whirring away over a cornfield out of range of a careless sportsman. But now, now I expect less of myself, and I do what I can do. You can't love me in return? I love you, Maribel, as a daughter. Oh, I said, how awful. I warned you I might sound fatherly. And I said, and my face was beginning to disperse, an eyebrow flew into one corner of the room, my nose perched on a chairback, my mouth scuttled under the bed like a mouse, my eyes fell into my hand and they felt so slippery I threw them out of the window while my voice, that voice, rose on a lark's wing of laughter resounding from the prettily painted ceiling, stars and the zodiac between beams, my voice sang, but I know no one like you, no one I like being with more, no one who's made me feel more myself, no one, I know I express myself badly, when will you go? Soon, he said, as if he hadn't noticed I was everywhere about him, after our play is performed, Maribel. I see, I said, and I could. All the bits of me were in place again but stiffly so, as if I'd been modelled by someone else who didn't really know who I was meant to be. What will I do when you're gone? this reconstructed booby asked. Still he didn't notice my different state. I don't know, Maribel, how can I? No, of course, you can't, this new me said with a tinkling, I almost wrote laugh but it was more like an articulated smile, but I do, the bright smile said, I know exactly what I'll do. What? Wait, I smiled triumphantly. Wait for what? Wait to be disenchanted, just like your Dulcinea needs to be. Oh, he said, and his voice had never sounded sadder. Will you ever let her appear as her true self? I don't know, Maribel, I haven't decided yet. Oh, I see. I really shall have to wait then, shan't I?

The play began with the knight and squire riding through the audience and up the flight of steps to the west terrace. Rocinante like Chica refused the steps but the donkey didn't mind them so the squire dismounted and helped push the horse from behind while the knight pulled on the bridle. All four parts were played by the same four players and this beginning was much the same, thanks to the animals' interpretation of their roles, as Marco's Masque of Merlin, but without the gunfire and trumpets. As before it proved to be a good start, causing ripples of indulgent laughter. We and the audience were seated below the terrace and behind us was a tower of wooden scaffolding hung with bamboo screens, secured by guy ropes and surmounted by an enormous head with staring eyes and a gaping mouth. The tower was the giant, Malambruno. From his huge red mouth, big as a cave, stretched ropes traversing the audience and secured to the stone balustrade which surmounts the west side of the house. At the house end were pulleys with more ropes hanging down from them. These arrangements had provoked much admiration and discussion among our guests before the performance. The tower-giant was surely a triumph of showmanship, a baleful painted bogy forty feet high. Marco's pride, and downfall.

The knight began the play with a formal address to

Jerónimo and me, begging hospitality and a period of rest from his labours. We both had a line each to say, as hosts, from our seats in the audience. Jerónimo said, no one deserves more honour than the renowned Don Quixote whose deeds ought to be recorded in brass, and I said, we were both word-perfect as ourselves, you are welcome, sir, but lo, who comes here? Whereupon, it was an important cue and I had to pitch my voice forward, the library doors opened behind our heroes and out trooped the countess with her twelve ladies-in-waiting, all heavily veiled in the eastern fashion so that their beards would get a laugh when revealed. The countess told her extraordinary story in a long speech which I'd said I was sure would stupefy the audience but in fact, it was most peculiar, everyone listened with serious, even rapt attention. I kept looking round as she spoke and on all sides I saw intent, absorbed faces. I caught his eye and he winked because he'd told me they would but I hadn't believed him, I'd said, who's going to listen to this fairy-tale nonsense at the very beginning of a play? And he'd said, because it's at the beginning, Maribel, and because a story is always a story however far-fetched doesn't matter so long as it trots along in an easy rhythm from incident to incident, is true to itself and hasn't got too many holes. Holes? I mean inconsistencies. Almost invariably when inventing a story you find there are some things which won't fit together and if they prove unbringable together, then instead of trying to close the gap it is best to quicken your pace, gallop through the hole with a flourish of tail and a flick of hooves. Perform some sort of trick? Yes, it's not ideal but very little is entirely ideal. The other thing is that at the opening of a play every playwright has an initial breeze of public goodwill to float on. Most people, ordinary people not critics, of course, want to like a play, why else have they come? This goodwill lasts in my experience, for about four minutes, the length of the countess's speech. After that, of course, the playwright must do something astonishing because people come to the theatre to be amazed, truly astounded. And when I say do something I mean it, action is everything in the theatre. Plays don't describe events, they are events, that's why they're so difficult to write. How he loved to talk about the theatre. And what do we do in order to amaze? I asked. We bring on the machinery, the horse, who else? Clavileño.[1] We had another long argument about the horse, well, about how it came to be where it was, since the countess had said it was the giant's horse and, now suddenly here it was being wheeled out of the library on to our terrace, all ready to transport our heroes. Well, that's what I mean by a hole, Maribel. We thought and thought and nothing we suggested convinced us. I watched dusk gather over the gardens and the river and finally I gave up racking my brain and lay back deliciously and simply watched him as he thought. He lit a candle and sat down again, quite straight, and behind his eyes I fancied I could see all kinds of landscapes and people and possibilities I had never known moving to and fro, meeting, dispersing, dissolving. A sort of changing weather in his mind. His lips were slightly parted, his face expressionless, its essential contours kind. He sat and sat. And that reminds me, when he did write he never frowned, he would sit first as I've described him, then when he was ready he would write very quickly, his small hand moving across the page, no pause for thought while he dipped his pen in the ink. His pens were curious, he trimmed almost all the feathers from them so there was just a little tuft left at the top like a lozenge. He'd wear them down to two-inch scraps. I've never seen anyone sharpen a pen so quickly. Where he'd sat writing would be surrounded with shavings. He always recorded his thoughts in their entirety, he never stopped in mid-sentence, never went back to correct, he composed complete paragraphs, whereas I, when I try to

[1] *Clavileño* means Wooden Peg, referring to the control mechanism in its head.

write, I keep stopping, crossing out, revising. He never did. We didn't solve the problem of the magic horse that evening but the following afternoon when he came to my room (that was the first time I was able to sit fully dressed in a chair) he said that it was simple. The giant sends the horse, Maribel, it is his horse so he sends it. But why and you haven't said you're glad to see me dressed and sitting up? But I am, Maribel. You look yourself again, quite perfect. Thank you, I said. I'm much thinner though, this dress used to fit me, now it's loose. And I showed him, pulling at the waist and bodice, I'm like a stick, Jerónimo hates thin women, my breasts are like empty purses, look. I think I hoped either to embarrass him by my frankness or to confirm the intimacy between us, I'm not sure which. I achieved neither. You'll soon be as you were before this illness, he said, to me you already are, and he took my hand and kissed it. So you do like me even though you can't love me? Why did I keep asking such baby questions? Why? It was much better between us when we just talked about the play, our play, his play. I'm sorry, I said, the effort of being dressed has made me stupid, tell me why the giant sends his horse? You're sure it won't tire you? No, just talk, it doesn't matter what you say, so long as you're with me and talking. How naive I was eight years ago.

The giant dwells nine thousand six hundred and eighty-one miles from your terrace so obviously in order to accomplish their victory our heroes need Clavileño. Quite, I said, quite. The countess announces the distance, the squire objects with his usual pragmatism and that is the time to drag the horse out of the library. All are astonished, you've seen Marco's designs for Clavileño, all is explained and that's the first scene, I've written it. He handed me the pages to read. The writing was neat, evenly spaced and every capital letter or small letter with a head or tail earned a flourish so he had had to leave quite a large space between his lines to accommodate them. His handwriting reminded me of his knight and squire: the lean, gesticulating, extraordinary one and the small, round, ordinary one progressing steadily down one page, then up and over to the next. While I was reading he said that what made it work was the distance. By stating an exact distance rather than a round ten thousand miles we created, he said, a split second of what I call spurious plausibility, Maribel, which, while the audience savours it, enables us to jump through the hole. It's still a cheat, I said, but he'd made me laugh. Oh, yes, but victims of a confidence trick often give the devil his due. They say, well, he fooled me but so cleverly, with such charm, I could almost forgive him. I still had doubts but in the event he was right, nobody minded, because the arrival of the horse was indeed what mattered. Get the horse on and we've won the first battle, Maribel. And we did, everyone loved the horse, it personified the absurdity of everything. It rolled out on a trolley steadied by eight burly peasants who were supposed to be noble savages. Clavileño's body was a huge wine barrel, his legs young birch trunks, his tail reeds from the river and his neck and head had been carpentered with relish by the local wheelwright. A spade handle between his leather ears was the apparent means of guidance. He had a most spirited expression, red-painted eyes, flaring nostrils and when at last he flew it could be seen that he was a stallion, albeit by the grace of papier mâché. His body was painted bright green and his legs were yellow. He was also rather worryingly heavy. The audience cheered with delight. They had entered into our childishness.

After much argument and explanation of the purpose and efficacy of the spade handle the knight and squire were persuaded to mount the beast. It was during this scene that the countess and her ladies lifted their veils to reveal their beards, another moment of general approval although I thought they looked more pathetic than funny but I expect that was me, I don't like deformities however incongruous, I have to look away from crippled beggars, I can't look and laugh, even though I know their defects are often self-inflicted or feigned. In Valladolid there is a courtyard known as the Court of Miracles where the beggars revert to their normal, healthy selves after a day's work.

The noble savages attached the ropes from the pulleys to Clavileño and we all held our breath, some of us looking up a little nervously, speculatively, at the other, tauter ropes overhead. I don't blame our audience, it did look a dangerous enterprise now. Whispers began, I hope they've tested this, it looks frightfully heavy to me, will the horse fall, daddy? No, but it might turn turtle. It had during rehearsal but Marco had solved the problem by having Clavileño's legs drilled and lead inserted to redress the balance. Then, there on the roof, lined up behind the balustrade, were seven magnificent trumpeters in livery blowing a fanfare and Clavileño with his riders was hauled into the air by the straining savages. I can't say it looked particularly magical but our contraption was becoming suspended between earth and heaven which was a luminous blue changing to violet with the evening star shining below the newest of new moons. Other pulleys, worked from the tower, now began to pull Clavileño across, away from the house. The horse didn't fly so much as slide and jerk in a lugubrious swoop, its sheer weight causing the overhead ropes to bend downwards. Behind us the tower-giant's scaffolding creaked and groaned ominously. Some people moved clear of their seats. At the lowest mid-point of the journey it stopped and a slightly strained dialogue ensued some ten feet above our heads. The heroes, and nobody doubted their heroism now, discussed their where-abouts in the sky and there was a terrible but lovely wobbly moment when the squire improvised, the conceited kitchen boy exulting in his role, saying he wanted to get off, they had flown so high they had reached Heaven, and he wanted to go and play with some pretty goats he could see grazing on the well-kept lawns. Marco insisted he couldn't get off, they were nowhere near Heaven, and he pointed to the moon as proof, saying, look, son Sancho, we haven't yet passed the horns of the moon. Our guest used that extempore dialogue with marvellous effect later. The trumpets blew again, the knight wiggled the spade handle and they moved on and upwards in a slow, tantalising curve towards the tower until at last they reached their destination, the giant steadied, the audience sighed with relief and they were swallowed up by Malambruno's gaping jaws. Great applause.

They appeared next on top of the giant's head, the topmost platform of the tower. Another fanfare to mark this triumphant moment, after which the knight announced that the giant was vanquished and the spell lifted. Water from buckets was poured out of the giant's eyes and ran down his cheeks. The countess and her ladies unhooked their beards, more cheers, and the two lovers, destatuefied, came out from the bottom of the tower and progressed in all their warm humanity, hand in hand, through the audience to the terrace. Marco had wanted the heroes to fly back again but one flight had been enough even for him and so he and his squire returned on foot to general acclaim and, joy of joys, the horse playing Rocinante whinnied in delight. This entertainment which in the telling has sounded as coyly contrived as it actually was, restored me, at least, to happiness. It ended with an epilogue to the effect that no one could tell whether the knight and squire had dreamt their exploit or really experienced it. The audience called back, they did, we saw it and suffered it with them. Laughter. I don't know who was more relieved that there had been no accident, the performers or the audience. The pantomime's machinery was undoubtedly the most extravagant that Marco had ever contrived. It was shortly after this that Jerónimo dismissed him for neglect of his household duties. He now manages a theatre in Madrid. Then our guest left.

I begged him to stay longer, I sulked, swore I'd go with

96

him, I even faked another illness or rather a relapse but he saw through my pretence and told me plainly, too plainly I thought, that I was as strong as Clavileño. After he left I wrote dozens of letters to him. He replied to the first three very pleasantly but after that my messenger came back empty-handed. Gradually the gap in my heart closed but it took a long time. Perhaps his wife saw my letters and became jealous? He would never tell me anything about her however much I asked. All I knew was that she was called Catalina. I assumed he did not love her but that may have been a delusion.

Friday 25th February

I shall leave before—

At this point in the MS the diary breaks off and the next few pages are occupied by accounts of expenses incurred on a journey: charges for accommodation, the hire of horses, estimates of the resale value of items of jewellery, payment of an armed escort referred to as F. The diary begins again in unconnected mid-sentence, indicating that some pages are lost, either torn out while still bound or mislaid once the book was broken up. The next entry to carry a date, 31 March, also records the place where it was written, Tudela, a town on the river Ebro. One internal reference gives a tantalising glimpse of a single but material event during this unchronicled month: María Isabel's escape from the convent.

—come completely into its own as a mausoleum for dead animals. The rain drummed against the shutters and already the house smelt of damp although it couldn't have been empty for long. I went slowly up the stairs, my body felt so heavy, and along the corridor to my rooms. They were locked. I came back to the head of the stairs and called down to Juana in the hall below. She hated being in the house at all, had refused to come up with me. She went to fetch Pedro. She was a long time. While she was gone

I went to the apartment which he had occupied so long ago. The doors here were open. His bedroom, his study. Anonymous guest rooms, no character, no life. There was half the shell of a pigeon's egg lying on the hearth in his study. I remembered what his knight said when he was dying, after the squire had told him not to, that the stupidest thing a man could do was to die and why couldn't he get up so they could go and look for Dulcinea again, and, who knew, they might find her, under some hedge, looking like herself? And the knight told him never to look for the birds of this year in last year's nests. It's an old proverb, I believe.

When Pedro arrived he was wet through and grumbling, saying he hadn't been left the keys for her ladyship's rooms, they were new locks his lordship had had put on and it was more than his job was worth to try and force them. Eventually I persuaded him (oh, the effort to summon up arguments at all) saying I would write a special letter which he could give to the duke when he returned and in it I would say that the forcing of the locks had been my responsibility alone, not his. But he said you were dead, my lady? He was speaking poetically, Pedro, you know, when people exaggerate, when they don't really mean you to take what they say as true? Still he doubted me, as he'd done when we first called at the lodge, but his wife had been with him then and she hadn't doubted me. I'm still me, Pedro, your wife knew who I was, didn't she? He nodded reluctantly. I'm not a ghost, feel. I held out my hand, he touched it. You don't look the same, my lady, you never used to wear a shawl on your head. Times and fashions change, Pedro. I didn't show him my newly sprouting hair, that would have sent him scuttling down the stairs. Please, Pedro, please believe me. In the end he left to fetch his tools. Another wait. I persuaded Juana to come up and we went through other rooms, one opening on to another. Jerónimo had removed most of the furniture from his. Clearly he didn't intend to live again in my house for some time, if ever. Was it still my house? Who could say what his lawyers would arrange if the annulment he was seeking succeeded. Perhaps it already had? How long do such things take? I don't know. It didn't feel like my house any more, it was a dull place, a dead thing shrouded in rain, marooned in slush. From a window at the back I looked out: the river had over-flowed its banks, the naked poplars stood in water which had invaded the meadows as far as the gardens where already several pools gleamed inside the clipped box hedges, curious intricate frames for liquid-looking glasses. But I felt almost nothing so I knew I was in control of myself.

The doors had to be smashed before we could enter. Inside was a bloodless shambles. Someone had damaged everything he could reach, had pulled the tapestries from the walls, overturned the bed, with what strength? It was immensely cumbersome, it lay on its side, in pools of crimson curtains like a four-legged monster. Someone, only Jerónimo, had knifed cushions and pillows, feathers were everywhere, had even cracked the tiles with a hammer or axe. Diana lay broken, headless, bowless. Her pedestal stood however. And there was the book, his history, broken-backed, the pages torn out, scattered everywhere. My first impulse was to gather them up but I didn't, I realised the absurdity in time. I stepped across my room as if crossing a street, curfewed after a riot. In my dressing room the mirror was a sad starburst of splinters, my clothes, torn from closets and chests (I had hoped for fresh ones), were a heap of half-charred rags and there were scorch marks on the side of the travelling coffer my father had given me when I was married. Jerónimo must have attempted to set fire to my things, had second thoughts perhaps, or else the servants had come and drenched the flames despite their master's frenzy. I did feel something now, relief, which was a release from obligation, and pity, not much but some, for Jerónimo. Behind those dead letters of his had been this rage, this paroxysm of sadness and a living

99

incomprehension.

Did you know about this? I asked Pedro. The old man grunted, not wishing to answer, still fearful of my extinct authority. Did you? No, my lady, nobody said in so many words. He was half-lying, innumerable words must have been spoken as he'd admitted, they would have flown all over the province. But what, fact or rumour? What did the duke do, apart from this, Pedro? Well, he gave parties for a while, he never asked no women, just men. I could imagine those parties. Then he shut himself in. Next thing we know he orders the house to be cleared, he had eight wagons for the furniture, they say they're still stuck in the snow south of here on the road to Zaragoza but I can't say about that. Anyway he goes, a fortnight back. And the servants? Oh, he began dismissing them just after Epiphany, my wife was worried sick but he kept me on, caretaker he said I was. You don't have a mind to stay, your ladyship? No, where would I sleep? That was my meaning. But it's too late for me to go any further tonight. You wouldn't get nowhere, my lady, the weather's against you.

So I'm writing this in the west lodge, in Pedro's and Luisa's bedroom, after garlic soup, some cheese and two glasses of red wine. I'm sleepy. Why are some people so kind while others are so—? I can't write cruel really because it's more complicated than that, they act in accordance with their convictions, that's closer to what I mean. Luisa insisted I should have their room and has recommended goose grease to make my hair grow quickly. She apologised for giving me the best she had, kept smiling and patting my arm and told me five times I was no trouble. Folks say you're crazy, my lady, but I believe what I choose to believe, to listen to some you'd think the world was never right. So I am cosseted and yawning my head off but I must record the good news. I can continue my journey. When I pressed the criss-cross centre of the carved marigold in the side panel, the bottom of the ransacked coffer sprang up as it was meant to do and there were my old treasures. Rings, some gold Mexican trinkets, a tiny crystal skull on a silver chain, a string of pearls, an emerald bracelet and a velvet purse with twelve heavy gold coins inscribed Philippus DG Hispaniarum et Indiarum Rex 1591.[1] This is enough for Juana and me to travel with and even live on for a while, afterwards, if I'm careful, that is. I tell myself I must be careful, I must think of myself as poor, which I am, and because I don't really know the value of these things and I'm certain to be cheated on the way and in Madrid, the city I hate but which contains him or at least news of him. I must go to bed now.

I don't know the day, I've lost count and Pedro doesn't know either, he thinks it's a Thursday. We're marooned. I can't even begin my journey but I'm determined to be patient because now I have no one to blame for my imprisonment except God whose rain still falls outside. I shan't blame Him. All round are floods. We wouldn't even reach the village, Pedro says. I can't see the house from here, it's curtained off by silver greyness. But I'm warmer here than I was in the hunting lodge, let alone in the woodpile outside the kitchen, waiting, waiting until dawn for Juana and the farmer's sledge.[2]

I've been back to the house once to collect his book. I'm putting it in order, it seems most of it will make sense now except for some half-pages near the end. Each time I see the duchess mentioned my determination increases but I no longer feel desolated or outraged. My indignation is strong and coherent now.

Thursday 31st March

At Tudela. I've seen the world and it is horrible. A moment

---

[1] Owing to inflation such older coins were worth more than their face value.

[2] This reference is the only indication of how María Isabel escaped from the convent. Presumably she concealed herself until the arrival of the farmer and Juana with logs for the convent kitchens.

ago a little ratlike boy crept into this kitchen. He didn't see me at first but when he did he darted away. People are vermin, there is no other word for them, lascivious vermin. I hate them, hate them, Juana too! God preserve me. It's all very well to read about such people but actually to meet them! They smell, well, of course I knew that, but when you're forced to be close to them their proximity smells, smells! They've got no human sensibilities at all except the day before yesterday's food still stuck between their teeth. And to be forced to listen to them, to endure their conceit, their repulsive satisfaction with their own ignorance. Yes, I knew all this, too, but now I've met them and must be part of them. They use proverbs like polished truncheons to hit you over the head! Folk wisdom, folk lore, is a rotted mouth guffawing at anything less bestial than itself. I'm not real to them because they are so busy being real to themselves. I cannot think what Christ meant when he said the lowly shall inherit the earth, he must have been off his head! I feel I want to write to someone about it, to protest to someone who has the power to do something! These people walk about the world as if it belonged to them! I vomited on the stairs but at least the man slipped on the mess and then fell down the rest. I wish he were dead instead of snoring in the hall. He said he was a graduate of Salamanca University but that didn't stop him being a libidinous, drunken peasant.

It must be nearly dawn, please God let it be nearly dawn, there's no church clock near enough to tell me, which is peculiar because I'm in the middle of this frightening town. The best hotel, they assured us. Jerónimo wouldn't have stabled a mule in it. Please let it be dawn. That boy who came in, he must have been supposed to do something in this kitchen ready for the morning. Kill the cockroaches perhaps?

We waited four days for the rain to stop, then three more for the floods to subside. Pedro borrowed a horse and cart from the village and drove us in what I now realise was comfort, as far as the bridge. Twenty miles of gluey mud and when at last we reached the stone bridge it was broken. On the other side of the swollen river we could see the town huddled on its knoll in the dusk like a shepherd wrapped against the weather in a plaid of dun, russet, grey. The broken bridge looked strange, it had grown a drowned forest on the upstream side where whole winter trees, brushwood and driftwood had been pressed against it by the flood. The mud-stained, weed-encrusted debris towered over its narrow causeway. But water poured through the broken middle arch with the force of a huge mill-race.

There was a ferry to take Juana and me across but the cost was prodigious, one of my precious gold pieces, so already I've been cheated. I wished that Pedro could come with us but he had been kind enough already and was anxious to get home. So Juana and I stepped out of the boat and into the town alone. The ferryman refused to help us with the travelling chest. Before we found this place we had gathered a following of emaciated children and furtive, speculative youths who escorted us mostly from behind, although occasionally a knot of them would dart up the narrow, stepped street ahead and then look back with blank eyes at two women walking alone and carrying their own luggage between them. I know now what they assumed us to be.

The landlord thought so, too. A narrow exclamation mark of a man, full of angrily snapping jocularity; the good humour of forty years strained through a sieve of rancour finely woven out of the conflicting demands of countless clients; an essentially lazy man whom life, or a wife, had forced to be always busy. At first there was no room for us, then there might be if we didn't mind sharing with two other ladies at which he looked us both up and down in order to stress the term. I hadn't thought of Juana like that before, but clearly this world did. These other *ladies* never arrived. They must have been whores with discrimination.

I accepted and he took us up to the place. I think it had been a granary, there were open rafters under a steeply pitched roof, no windows and a smell of bats. Four straw palliasses and dirty blankets completed the amenities. What a fool I was! I said, you don't expect us to sleep here, do you? No, he replied with a grin, but I dare say you'd like somewhere to operate from? I pretended not to understand him. We've got better beds, of course, but they're reserved for the gentlemen. It's cash in advance here and you won't be able to afford a real bed until tomorrow morning, will you? So you pay for these now and enjoy the gentlemen's beds to their satisfaction and your profit, don't you? And he winked. This way we both benefit, don't we? But I told you who I am. Yes, yes, he said, you're a lady travelling incognito with her maid, you all say that. I didn't argue with him. I paid in advance, he seemed pleased with the gold coin I gave him which proved that the ferryman had overcharged me. Only ten left and I've hardly begun my journey! He left saying, more obsequiously now, that he'd send up our luggage but it never came. I lay down. I didn't cry. I'd expected to cry. I lay and stared at the rafters, the cobwebbed tiles. Juana said I would feel better after supper.

Certainly she did. I hadn't wanted to go down but she persuaded me. She came to life in that crowded room where the fire smoked continually. We sat together at a long table. Soon we were flanked and fronted by gobbling, guzzling men. No gentlemen had arrived, that was obviously a fiction of the landlord. These men ate with their hands or from knives or scooped with wads of bread and they drank from the jug, jutting out their lips like leather beaks. They talked over and across each other, words and food masticated together, projecting opinions, prejudices, judgements interlarded with disgusting jokes addressed to each other, Juana and me, as if we were like them. My eyes were smarting, I couldn't breathe, I couldn't hear myself think, but Juana began to laugh, drink, drank more at their insistence, talked back, began to shout, became raucous, dismissive of me and at last squealed delightedly when someone pawed her leg. The food was some kind of vegetable stew in which a pig's trotter swam in each bowl. How they gnawed at the cloying fat clinging to those knuckle bones, how the grease dribbled from their chins and slurped to solidity on the table among the breadcrumbs and spilt wine. When I got up they all laughed. Wasn't their company good enough for her ladyship? I begged a candle from one of the serving girls and found my way back up the turning stairs. I didn't sleep. I decided to return home the next day to my dead house by the river. Better to live in loneliness than endure such insult from the loose-lipped world. But Juana could stay, stay where she belonged, here, I no longer required her services, oh no, to think that Juana, my Juana, who'd been so loyal, so loving, so chaste, could change like that ! One touch of the world and she belonged to it. I hadn't been able to believe what I was seeing, hearing. She enjoyed their jokes, their suggestions, their leering propositions. She was another person, Juana. And they liked her, wanted her, her dwarf body, ugly hands, snub nose, squinty eyes. There was so much left for me to learn, be taught. The straw in the mattress creaked under me, rustled with what seemed an existence of its own. I hadn't moved. Mice? I was too contemptuous to care and I've never minded mice, anyway. But I did feel dirty lying in my clothes. Finally I slept, swaddled in revulsion and self-pity. I couldn't bring myself to use the blankets provided.

Until now I've spared myself and these pages some aspects of what I've experienced, either through modesty or timidity, I don't know; but now in this kitchen I feel, I'm shivering with cold again, I feel I must be accurate, can I be, it was only a few hours ago?

Huge shadows looming, dancing hobgoblins, giant shadows and whisperings, moanings, cryings and a weight against me and something nibbling at my skirts, my neck, my bodice. A sudden chorus of laughter, drunken voices and I was awake and I saw Juana crouched on her hands and knees on the mattress next to mine and, oh God, she was being tupped, no other word for it, like a shorn sheep by a pot-bellied peasant with his breeches round his ankles and his hands gripping her shoulders, his thighs thin and knotted while Juana, her face upside down, transported by pleasure, was laughing and crying all at once and beyond her I saw cadavers with demon eyes. The next moment I realised they were men whose faces were lit from below by a lantern set down on the boards and this, what was this? This squirming substance on the other side of me, clawing inside my skirt, mauling at my stomach, pulling at my buttocks, its fingers digging into me trying to open my legs with sharp nails which gouged and scratched? I screamed, kicked, rolled off the palliasse. More giant laughter. Why? I staggered upright and saw why. The creature, thing, that had assaulted me was kneeling, both hands to his groin, exclaiming in pain. He looked up and I recognised him as the man who'd sat opposite me at supper, who'd tried to impress me with snatches of Latin which even I knew made no sense. Words came out of his contorted, baboon-bottom face, you wait, you bitch, you cow, its enflamed puckeredness emitted. But I didn't wait, I ran, except the watching demons caught me, shouting whoa, hey-up, and I was held. And in that instant of immobility with every man's hand on me, *me*, every breath in the room enveloping me in garlic, wine, caries, I saw Juana fall face forward in the final realisation of her lasciviousness and the man rocking back on his heels laughed to see the convulsions rack that heap of flesh in front of him. The men who held me laughed too. I shut my eyes and heard that other voice of mine whispering hard at me, above my head somewhere, saying nonsensically, think, be careful, they'll turn on you next. I struggled, screamed again and the man I kicked got up and came towards me, this man, this baboon, this graduate of Salamanca who'd boasted of his translations of Ovid, Lucretius and his prowess with women, this man came towards me! Hold on to her, he said, her ladyship kicks like a mule.

106

Please, I said, I'm not what you think I am, I am what I say I am, please! Turn her round, he said. Why? Why? And they obeyed him, they turned me round and I felt his hand tug at the back of my dress, I heard buttons plip plop plip on the bare boards, that was why, and still my unreal voice called, be careful, think, Maribel, because if this uncouth person succeeds in his intentions there'll be nothing left for you, you couldn't live afterwards, you'll have to kill yourself, you realise that, I'm sure. And I thought why, why did he pretend, that author we entertained, why did he tell me the world which I've met now, can feel now, its hands are all over me, why did he say, why, that this world is good, is kind, at worst is farcical? Why? Why?

Because he was right. Because Juana proved him right and so did the landlord who appeared at the same moment as Juana returned to her senses and shouted, no, stop! And the landlord shouted something, too, so that everyone turned and their enormous hands on me were loosened and, thank God I had enough wits left to run, then and there, to push past the landlord at the head of the stairs and to continue down, down. My stomach was churning and at the first turn I had to stop and be sick. Above me there was more shouting and the sound of boots clomping in what seemed to be some sort of cloddish country dance and even as I vomited I realised that the landlord's coming had saved me, me, a damsel in distress, real distress, saved by a thin, middle-aged man who ought not to have been wearing an apron but rusty armour with a brass barber's basin as his helmet. And he ought to have looked like him, like his author, only impossibly elongated, as if he'd been painted by that expatriate Greek who lived in Toledo.[1] Then I ran on down with my persecutor clattering after me until he slipped, fell headlong and shot past me as if the remaining stairs were a helter-skelter, and lay still.

The landlord apologised, made me as comfortable as he

[1] Clearly El Greco. If only he had painted Cervantes's portrait; they were contemporaries.

could in the kitchen, brought my luggage, poked up the fire, offered me a glass of brandy. He said, you see, madam, we get all sorts here, it's a passing through sort of place, Tudela. I said I quite understood. Do I?

There's light, grey light creeping into the room now so it really is morning at last and despite no sleep at all I must think of practical things such as how to accomplish the next stage of my journey more sensibly because I'm aware in this dawn that I cannot go back. My author must, in all honour, tell me the truth. He must give me myself back. He must do that. It is what I intend but I shan't take Juana. Here she is.

Friday 1st April

At Tarazona. First I must admit I already miss her. One day gone and I miss her! Me, who only this morning was implacable. My virtue has been rewarded exactly as her lack of it was. I feel less and less proud of myself. Life's dispensations, it seems, are measured out more accurately than I thought.

However, I travelled here in lovely peace of mind, or was it selfish security? The countryside shone, the hoof-beats rang on the icy road, there were diamonds on every tree and frosted fields under a sky clear of cloud until evening. My companions were friars returning to their friary at Veruela a little to the south from here. Gentle, discreet persons who have established a hospital in Pamplona, who believed me when I said I was me and requested permission to travel with them. They didn't laugh or joke or ask why I was travelling alone. They hardly said anything at all. But they did recommend this house as a refuge for me. It belongs to the local priest, an elderly rheumaticky man who is celebrating vespers at the moment so I'm alone in his study. He has a number of books.

Juana begged to be forgiven. She showed me money, saying, you see, madam, I earned my keep, I haven't stayed here at your expense. She said madam, not Miss Maribel,

108

which shows the gulf that had opened between us. I was stone, I would not, could not forgive her for enticing those men. She protested that she was forced to do what she did. She insisted I didn't understand how it had begun as harmless banter no worse than what could often be heard in the kitchens of my own house. How it had grown from that into foolishness of food, company, warmth, wine until it was too late. I told her I had no wish to recall any instant of that dreadful occurrence. What a hypocrite I was, hadn't I just sat up all night recording it? I told her to pursue her new profession alone. She backed away from me then, her face blotched by fear and shame and fury. I only did what's natural, madam, I'm a grown woman like you, do you suppose because I'm ugly I have no desires? Thou art hard and cruel! I didn't answer, I was too exhausted. She followed me crying to the town gate. But I didn't relent and I didn't look back as I rode away. So now I miss her. And I wonder if it is ever possible to be both just and kind?

This priest hasn't read *Don Quixote* which is a marvellous relief, suppose he'd recognised me? He's heard of the book, of course, one of his parishioners recommended it to him but he never reads novels, he says, history, yes, some classic poets, I'm afraid I stop at Horace really. He's a nice man, a little snobbish, I think, so I've lied to him, told him I'm travelling to join my husband, the Duke, in Madrid. Naturally he's puzzled that a duchess should be travelling alone so I've told him, fabricating upon truth, that I dismissed my servants, what a difference the plural rather than the singular makes in such conversations, for misbehaviour. We had a long, slightly high-pitched, dismissively laughing discussion about the unreliability of servants nowadays but I could sense that he was still puzzled, if not suspicious. Didn't I think it dangerous to travel by myself? And uncomfortable? At this season of the year? And without a coach of one's own? I told him it was simply a matter of not being impatient, of waiting at each stage of the journey for suitable companions to arrive, such as the party of Franciscans who'd escorted me here. Also that I found it intriguing to view the world more closely than I usually did, rather as our youthful aristocrats do, who dress up as shepherds for the make-believe fun of it, for the delicious rough and tumble of the simple life. I shouldn't have mentioned this; he was full of disapproval of this persistent trend in modern youth. It may be fashionable, he said, for the young to criticise the structure of society by their tomfoolery but it causes discontent. Why, we had a party of students turn up here last summer, they'd been sleeping under hedges, bathing in the river, encouraging the local girls to do the same and some had, playing guitars under the moon, helping with the harvest for half a day until the local people had become most indignant and rightly so, your ladyship. They'd come to him shocked and protesting, saying it was all very well for these rich young gentlemen to pretend to be like them, but they weren't and they ought to know their place. And he agreed. One should never confuse the poor, he said. So he thinks I'm eccentric and little better, no, worse since I'm female, than those students. But the fact that I'm a duchess weighs more with him than anything I do or say so he remains deferential and kind. He assures me that a local gentleman will be setting out for Madrid shortly and that he will be delighted to effect an introduction so I may travel with him.

There's a lovely mountain to be seen from my window. It's called Moncayo. I'd like to be up there in the snow at sunrise. Father Diego says one can climb it once the snow has melted but that won't be for a long time yet because spring comes late to these high hills. I feel incredibly well, physically I mean. I'm certain I'm fatter and every breath I take seems to energise me. My hands and feet stay warm all the time and if one could dance in this sober house I would.

The local gentleman is delightful. He's positively pretty. Don Rufo de Paz, aged twenty-three, blond curls! He says he owes them to his Milanese grandmother. He has an infectious laugh which bubbles out of him so frequently that you start to feel everything is as pretty and funny as he is. He laughs at almost everything I say. It does make a difference. When did I last have anyone to laugh with? His mother is a widow, he's very fond of her. She questioned me about my hair which has become a curious kind of fuzz about two inches long all over. I told her I'd had ringworm. I'm getting very good at lying. Rufo plays the lute very well and composes his own songs, mostly new words to old tunes. His mother tells me he will be perfectly safe to travel with.

Rufo has read the book, of course, but he didn't recognise me in it and I haven't said a word. Well, I almost did, but I stopped myself in time and said instead that I had met the author, I couldn't resist saying that, I said he was rather a friend of mine really and I hoped he would call on me in Madrid. You've met Cervantes! he exclaimed, you've met Miguel de Cervantes Saavedra?

There! I've written it. I've actually enscribed my chimera's name, I thought I never could, never would be able to allow my hand to do it, that's the influence of Rufo, for whom nothing is serious, I who had sworn to myself that I would never write it down partly because, because what, what? Why? Because I was never going to add to his fame, I suppose that was the stupid idea, not even in a private journal would he be shown to be of importance to anyone, which was absurd because anyone would have known whom I meant anyway. So why? I can only answer, derangement and pride. If I look back in this diary and I do sometimes I tell myself I am not to be tempted to change a word and I haven't because it's important to me that my diary records me precisely as I am, was, without the benefits or glosses of hindsight I seem to be forgetting punctuation again but I don't care because it doesn't matter now that I've written his name and if I'm short of breath it's only because I'm writing so quickly and the room isn't beginning to expand or dissolve and this page isn't shrivelling up as I thought it would and that other Maribel isn't saying anything, anything at all. Quite silent.

The peerless damsel remained three days in the good priest's house until the fair young knight was ready to depart. Aurora had clothed herself in her brightest hues— No, I won't be party to such rubbish. But I shan't cross it out neither as Juana used to say. Juana! Oh dear, I wish I didn't remember her. No, it shall remain, this nonsense sentence, as a memento-cum-signpost such as you sometimes see by the roadside erected in memory of someone in order to point the way for others who pass by. But now it's time to stop, it's supper time, I'm hungry, the sun has set behind Moncayo and I'm happy, yes, because that other me has gone, she's had her say and gone, can it be? And tomorrow I leave with funny Rufo for Madrid where I shall root out him, Miguel de Serpientes.

Wednesday 13th April

Forward and back, forward and back. I've had to revise my opinion of the world yet again. How dare it contain so many contradictions? It's a conspiracy, a deliberate conspiracy. No sooner do I learn to manage as other people do so easily than the world turns round and bites me.

I hardly have the will to go on, either with this journey or this diary. I tell myself I must, I must, you've nothing else left, Maribel, but I'm tired and feel twelve years older not twelve days. That silly signpost sentence I wrote had a kind of prescience in it, I don't mean its convoluted worn-out words but its direction. I accept the way it pointed. This happened to a person other than myself, no, no, I shall record it as if it hadn't really happened at all, not at all, as sheer fiction. I refuse to be involved ever again, enough is enough!

The first day of her journey passed without incident. The coach was comfortable, well, as comfortable as the road allowed and it was almost warm thanks to a brass bowl full of glowing charcoal. Her conversations with her recently acquired travelling companion were agreeable, the weather hard and clear. They reached the town of Olvega by early evening and spent the night with cousins of Rufo. A pleasant supper and early to bed. The next morning they set off at nine o'clock taking the road for Almenar de Soria eighteen miles away. (I like the tone of this, it is as mildly unremarkable as the experience was.) What made the journey so satisfactory to Maribel was its superficiality. She surrendered entirely to inconsequential sensations: the jolting, Rufo's chatter, the reassuring security of his four armed outriders, the continuing blueness of the sky. She even viewed the bludgeoning of a surly, importunate beggar with equanimity. Yes, do keep him away, she thought, nothing must interrupt our progress, my progress. Rufo congratulated the guards upon their prompt action. They spent the night at a comfortable inn in Almenar and how different it was from that other place in Tudela where Maribel had suffered indignities no gentlewoman should be expected to experience. Before she slept she did find herself remembering her maid but she pushed the thought aside as if it were one pillow too many.

A yellowing sky threatened snow the next day but Rufo was determined to go on. He lived only for the thought of reaching Madrid which he adored. They had already enjoyed many a teasing disputation upon the merits and demerits of that city. Maribel insisted it was an awful place. Then why are you going there? Because I must, as a dutiful wife, and her voice trilled with laughter which echoed his. How carefree she felt. She was almost prepared to believe her own lies, that she was indeed travelling to Madrid to join her husband whom she described to Rufo in glowing terms as an enormous man of inestimable talents, flowing wit, implacable courage. Rufo giggled at her description and said he sounds too good to be true, is he a passionate man? To her considerable surprise she found her tongue was loosened yet further, heard herself describing the most intimate details of her married state

113

as the snow began to fall. To listen to her, and how she listened to herself, already the sounds of the horse's hooves and the coach's wheels were muffled, the casual eavesdropper would have been embarrassed by the sudden looseness of her speech. Her falsehoods knew no limit as the huge snowflakes swirled ever more thickly until she and Rufo were enclosed in that leather and brocade cubicle like twins in a cradle no longer rocked by an unseen nurse.

The door opened and the coachman announced that they could go no further. He feared for the horses, he said, and he respectfully upbraided Rufo for refusing to stop at the last village. But it was a collection of hovels, answered Rufo, shut the door, I can't think with you staring at me. The coachman withdrew into the blizzard. She could hear him outside conferring with the guards, then the sound of the horses being unharnessed and the creak of the shafts as they were lowered to the ground. Rufo grew petulant now, demanded of Maribel what he should do? How I loathe weather, he said, it's so irrelevant to one's life! We must ride back to the village, she replied. But he refused. No, we can't go back, it's too far and we'd die of cold. The door opened again and this time the coachman asked politely if he could enter so they might discuss their predicament more comfortably? Rufo was about to say no but Maribel forestalled him, said, please, it's better than letting the snow blow in. He squeezed in and sat opposite them, an apologetic, melting snowman urging permission to save the horses. Poor Rufo. He proved incapable of decision. But Maribel and the coachman found they agreed. The guards should try to lead the coach horses back, spend the night at the village and return in the morning. The coachman got out again to instruct them. Still the snow fell. And what happens to us? asked Rufo. We'll be warm enough here, we have food, charcoal in the brazier and the snow will keep us warm. But we could be buried alive! She laughed at him. She said, no, sheep survive in snow drifts, so can we. But who

114

will guard us? He was frightened now. The coachman, of course. We're to share this space with a servant? Dear Rufo, he can't stay outside all night. Rufo sulked but said nothing when the coachman climbed in again without, this time, requesting permission to enter.

They spent a curious night imbued with tedium, discomfort, speculation and farce. Hours of silence punctuated by sudden bursts of conversation about the state of the weather (still the snow fell), about the horses and the guards, would they have reached the village? Then a clumsy interlude in which they ate an improvised supper in the dark, hands bumping, sharp breadcrumbs from an unseen crusty loaf, wine from a shared, felt-for bottle. Fitful sleep followed but not for Maribel. To her surprise it was Rufo who snored, not the coachman. Rufo, who seemed to her more a gilded figurine than a person, groaned and wheezed like a pair of mildewed bellows. She did not know, at that time, that one purpose of his visit to Madrid was to consult a physician. Soon Maribel's chief concern became the increasing necessity of using the chamber pot in the close presence of these two men. Never had the answer to a call of nature sounded so loud, shroud the brass pot how she might with her skirts. She felt herself blush in the darkness. Eventually the snow ceased and a huge moon rose. Its light pervaded the inside of the coach, an acidulous illumination which revealed the chillness, dampness of their close condition. The charcoal died in its bowl at their feet. She watched the last ember fade like a glow-worm surprised by light. Despite herself she drew nearer to Rufo for warmth. He awoke with a jerk and a sudden flung-out arm of alarm which hit her nose so hard that her eyes watered. He apologised and then grumbled. She began to despise him for his lack of fortitude and so slept at last. Dawn came with the sound of digging. The guards had returned with a party of labourers from the village, grunting, red-faced men who shovelled the snow clear of the coach. The three of them got out stiffly. Maribel felt as if her head was floating above a body made of aching cardboard. The villagers had brought aqua vitae and two gulps of it made her dizzy, a third, drunk. She remembered very little of the next slow day.

They reached a real town by midnight, the last few miles of their journey made easier by a chain gang of prisoners who were clearing the road by torchlight. She remembered the look of them for a long time afterwards, men strung together like beads, iron collars chafing their necks, wielding spades in a concerted fury which moved mountains of snow as if it weighed nothing. It was difficult to believe they were real, these sweating, flame-lit puppets, except that one fell down dragging his immediate confederates on either side of him to their knees and Maribel laughed before feeling a choking sensation of shame as if an iron collar were biting into her own neck. Armed warders came running, a whip rose and fell but the fallen man did not get up.

Rufo's spirits rose as the lights of the town grew nearer. By the time they passed through the main gate and the coach wheels were grinding on cobbles he was his old self again, his brush with danger forgotten, life was once more as light and feathery as he had always insisted it was.

But he was wrong. At this last place they had a choice of roads. Rufo chose sensibly and wrongly.

I can't write any more as if this hadn't happened to me. No. I wish I could but I'm me and I can't and it did. This latest place was called Almazán, and to reach Madrid two roads were possible. One went by way of the Pass of Villasayas to Sigüenza, the other which was straighter and safer to Medinaceli. The highroad from Madrid to Zaragoza passes below Medinaceli. I can see it below me now. Rufo decided to take the safer road even though they said it was quicker to go by Sigüenza. I agreed with him.

We were trotting downhill through drizzle when on rounding a bend the coachman shouted, the coach skidded, the horses panicked and we slewed sickeningly into a ditch.

116

More shouts and the horses squealed and struggled. There were shots. I could see nothing because Rufo had fallen across me and we were both trying to right ourselves. Rufo pushed back, upwards, tried to open the door which was above our heads now. Eventually he flung it back and climbed out. I remember his kicking feet, so small, so immaculately booted. I heard him call, what's the matter? I pulled myself up after him but no sooner had I got halfway out than a rider seized me and threw me across his horse in front of him. I glimpsed a tree trunk lying across the road ahead, the figures of many men, mounted and on foot and then the horse cleared the tree. In that instant, however, I saw Rufo, bright kingfisher blue and black, fling himself bodily towards one of our attackers. His opponent seemed made of muddy leather and he held a pistol thrust forward stiffly at Rufo. It exploded in his hand and both Rufo and he fell back. I know now that Rufo was killed at once and that his murderer was wounded by the unreliability of his own firearm. I have been invited to see him executed but I shan't go. He was the leader and when his fellows saw him fall they ran away. But I knew none of this at that time, all I was aware of was the pounding of the horse, my head hanging beside its heaving foreribs, my eyes seeing its hooves driving into the mud.

Rufo lies in the chapel here, together with the coachman and one of the guards. I have been in to look at them. The bandits got nothing from their ambush. Apparently they are a notorious group, mixed-blood outlaws.[1] I've rewarded my rescuer, Francisco, who was one of Rufo's outriders, with my emerald bracelet. I suspect that this was over-generous of me, except he saved my life, of course.

I've written as best I could to Rufo's mother. Poor woman, she was very proud of him. My letter will reach her with his body. Everyone here looks to me for decisions

---

[1] *Moriscos,* many of whom were driven to banditry after refusing to obey the repatriation laws.

117

and I have been able to make them. I shall proceed in a few days' time with Francisco accompanying me while the other two guards will drive the coach containing the body back to Tarazona. The coachman and the guard have been buried here this morning. At my expense, which is a blow to me, although I see it is just. Everyone in Medinaceli tells me I was very lucky because the bandits are known to perform atrocities upon Christian women. They aren't gentlemen outlaws at all apparently, nothing like the courteous desperadoes one meets in novels. Miguel used to say no one is as bad as he is painted but he had sympathy for every kind of outcast, beggar, vagabond. A sort of idealised fellow-feeling authors often indulge in, I suppose. I must enquire about the hire of horses. Francisco thought we should borrow Rufo's but I was too proud to do that. What would his mother think of me?

Sunday 17th April

At Guadalajara. The city is full for the Easter celebrations. I have not been welcomed at the palace nor been invited to sit in a balcony to watch the tournaments and bullfights. I did wonder whether to present myself but who could I say I am? I'm no one now without Jerónimo. We used to know the Marquis of Guadalajara. He's a kindly person, rather vague and forgetful. I couldn't go to him as a beggar, the hem of my dress needs mending. I attended mass this morning and I saw a number of people from Zaragoza whom I recognised including Count Braja. How glittering he looked. I suppose I did once. I was tempted to wait for him outside the cathedral but in the end my courage failed me. I hurried away keeping my face covered. I must find a maid in Madrid, at least.

Monday 18th April

At Alcalá de Henares. They are very proud of him here. You can't speak to anyone without being told that the famous Cervantes was born in this quite pretty town. Like all Castilians they insist their town is full of marvels when in fact it is merely pleasant. Six persons have already gone out of their way to show me the house where he was born. It looks like any other house, four-square, modest. I shall reach Madrid tomorrow. There is no snow here. It's rather a relief. And the first storks have arrived.

Wednesday 20th April

Madrid. I dare not stir a foot from my lodgings. Francisco has gone. He wanted to stay but he knew I could not afford his wages. I confided in him a little but I never enlarged on who I was or what was the purpose of my visit to this city, which is bigger than I remember it. He was a most resolute companion on what remained of my journey. I shall miss him but not as much as I miss Juana whom I would take back if I ever saw her again.

I expected that I would make immediate enquiries about his whereabouts. After all he may not be here, he may be enjoying someone else's hospitality almost anywhere, writing his next masterpiece every morning, charming his next hostess every afternoon. Or he could be in Esquivias, his wife had a house there, I think. It's a day's journey from here but I don't want to travel again. If I must I will, I suppose, but I'd rather not. So I don't ask in case I'm answered either way, yes, he is here, no, he's not. So I sit.

I have a small room on the fourth floor of this house. It overlooks the main square. I was offered a room at the back, it was cheaper and quieter but I have to be able to look out. If I can't look out I don't feel I'm anywhere. Just how long I shall be able to afford this front seat at the theatre of the world is another matter. The habit of luxury is difficult to shake off. At the moment everything is: I'm not sure or, I don't ask or, I can't quite think until tomorrow.

There are more beggars than people to beg from in

the square. They hobble, they sit, if legless they lie or wheel themselves about on little carts and if they are women they offer themselves, of course. They seem cheerful, as if what they are and do is normal, acceptable. I've also noticed how they distinguish between the truly rich and the apparently rich, those who are in fact almost poor as the beggars themselves but pretend they are not. I suppose that's what I shall have to do? Afterwards. After I've seen him, I mean. This afternoon. There, that's a promise. The square is square with stone arcades under which everything is sold. Above it there's a marvellous sky of wild scudding clouds over glorious blue. Below it the cobbles, washed by rain, sparkle. If I dared go out with any confidence I think I should quite like Madrid, after all. It is intriguing. But I should need company, someone with me to keep all the people at a distance because within the stern geometry of this city humanity runs in such rivers of noise, such ceaseless clatter and babble of importunity; they're too alive, much too alive for me. I'm more comfortable here. One must be rich to resist and enjoy large cities. I keep expecting to see Jerónimo ride through the square. I would recognise him at once, I'm sure. But he hasn't appeared yet. Like him, he may not be here, of course. But if he did, what would I do? So I am glad he hasn't because I wouldn't know what to do. It would put me in an unbearable position. You can hire sedan chairs and porters in the arcade at the front door of these lodgings. All I need to do is go down and say take me to the house of the author of *Don Quixote* and I'm certain the porters would take me there at once. They know where everything is. But to do that I should first have to visit a pawnbroker, there are several of their frightening shops in the square. I will find courage soon. This afternoon. I shall take my Mexican trinkets and be cheated. What does it matter so long as I reach him?

I keep telling myself my chief fear is poverty, but is it? That fear is bad enough but behind it lies something else.

I've come so far, endured so much. No, that is an exaggeration, I've encountered the usual reversals of fortune most travellers find, no more; no less, I still grieve for Rufo, his bright laughter. But now, now I'm ready to accomplish my intention, I sit here writing or watching the square. I'll do anything rather than what I came for. But I know exactly what I'll do, and what I'll say, when I do see him. I have planned it in my head. I shall be very contained, cool-voiced, rather grand really. I shall tell him a little about my differences with Jerónimo, I shall imply that it began with a disagreement about his book but that I managed eventually to persuade Jerónimo to take no action against him, and we are reconciled now. I shall not mention my imprisonment in the hunting lodge or in the convent, of course. I shall make it seem that I have been his champion, I may even suggest, but only with the utmost delicacy, that I was a trifle disappointed that he did not choose to dedicate the book to me, especially as his stay with us was clearly such an inspiration to him. But I shall laugh that delicate reproof aside, with light composure, because I shall be very much the Duchess María Isabel. Who else? I shall naturally say that since I happened to be in Madrid, my husband now having an important post at Court, I have called to congratulate him upon his continued success and that if he still needs anything I hope he will allow me to supply it? I shall have to phrase that in such a way that he is bound to refuse, of course. Only very gradually, going softly and gently, as he would say, will I come to the crux. I shall point out that he has himself betrayed the otherwise consistent tone of his masterpiece in those chapters where his heroes visit a certain Duke and Duchess. I shall say I was amused, of course, by his blatant transmogrification of a reality I recognised but disappointed by what I can only describe as rather awkward intrusions of opinion and certain medical facts irrelevant to his theme and muddying to his prose. Authors are very tender, even he. It will hurt him far more if I point to defects in his

121

art rather than in his behaviour towards me. I shall say
I'm certain posterity will proclaim him a careless genius
who did not know his own worth. That's what I'll say, yes!

Thursday 21st April

In order to be utterly sure of my ground I have been
rereading those chapters in which I am portrayed. They
are not quite as shocking as I remember them but this
time I have been impressed by the poverty of his imagination. By which I mean the way he cannot think of anything,
invent anything for himself. Everything is second-hand,
he's just a pattern-maker using other people and events as
his raw materials. He even puts in our joke about his stockings, Father Gattinara is there, but I must admit he deploys
him to great effect, Jerónimo walks and breathes again,
and, of course, the masques we presented in his honour are
now used to astonish and bemuse his knight and squire.
How dare he batten on reality so? And Dulcinea is never
released from her bondage, oh no! That would be too
sugar-sweet an ending. As for his liquid sententiousness,
I'd forgotten how evasive it was, just as you think he's
about to commit himself—but I've said all this before, why
do I keep telling myself things I already know? I'm like a
child who only wants the same story from her nurse over
and over again. I used to. Yesterday I was so sure of what
I would say to him but now? Now I just want to see him.
And who knows, tell him the truth? Which is what, now?
What?

Saturday 23rd April

I saw him yesterday. He was dressed as a Franciscan.

They didn't want to admit me when I reached the house.
They didn't seem to appreciate what efforts it had cost me
to arrive at his doorstep in that narrow courtyard. To
them I was just another visitor. I had to insist, tell them

I was an old friend of his. How surprising it is when one's lies come true. I know I am an old friend of his, now.

One of the women led me upstairs. She could well have been his wife but she didn't say she was. She was a remote, rather suspicious person much younger than I had expected, if it were she. The woman opened the door and withdrew but she didn't quite shut the door behind me. I think she watched me from the landing. There were sounds from the street below, the rattling of a cart, a woman calling monotonously to a child who wouldn't come to her while she chatted relentlessly to some other people. There was a strange, sweet smell.

Candles had been placed at his head and feet. But a shaft of sunlight shone on his face from one of the closed shutters which was broken. It wasn't the room of a rich man or a poor man. It had the simplicity, orderliness of the medium. Half and half. His profile had become a curved knife, one of those semi-circular knives made to fit a bowl in which herbs or small vegetables can be finely chopped. That was my first thought.

My second was to apologise, to say I was mistaken, I'm sure I misunderstood you, I'm terribly sorry, I realise at last. Everyone was right except me. I knelt beside him. He lay on a sort of bench, not a bed. It was like a modest catafalque. I wanted to say, I've read your book again, I realise you didn't necessarily mean me at all except, except for that small, private detail. Why did you put that in? But I didn't say it because he was dead and because I knew I had already answered it for myself somewhere, I can't look back through these pages, but somewhere. Even if he'd been alive I knew I wouldn't have asked him. If his purposes had been quite other then, they were even more so now. I wanted to make him smile again, to tell him how I had given myself away at Epiphany, how I had myself announced to everyone that I was his creation, how I'd danced in frenzy on the dinner table. He would have liked the incongruity of that scene I made. I wanted to say

123

only come back and you can use it in your next book, I don't mind, only come back, I realise now I'm any duchess and Jerónimo is any duke but I've lost him as I've lost you, and I wanted to tell him about the sparrow in my room behind Jerónimo's tapestry from Flanders which, do you remember, I told you about but you never mentioned it? Why not? I wish I'd taken you to see our hunting box. I wanted to say if you thought Father Gattinara was dreadful, and clearly you did, you should have met the peg doll, you would have made minced meat of him. Please come back and I'll tell you everything, about Chica in the kitchen, that must go into your next book, please, you have my permission to transform everything about me into gold, I'll tell you anything you want to know because I see how absurd it all was, I was. Please! And tell me, what did you die of? It can't have been just old age, someone like you doesn't die of that! You can smile really, I know you can. Can't I baby you as you babied me? Look at my hair, oh, you ought to have seen the convent, you who love mad people. My hair looks strange now, I know, but it looked even funnier a few weeks ago, I travelled here especially to see you, to tell you that you were quite right, absolutely and impossibly right as you always were, please smile. I think I was crying but only a little, looking at his stillness, remoteness, that once kind face whose eyes were shut.

There was peace in that room, that peace of God which is so purged of everything human, so set, that words like forgiving or unforgiving have no meaning. He was already his own memorial as everyone becomes, as I would be. I understood then, his very latest lesson, he could be a bit of a pedagogue, that when you meet someone dead you don't meet him but yourself.

I stopped crying. There was no need for me to cry. I might have expected to be angry. I think I should have been a month or so ago, to have felt cheated of a last interview but, no, his peace was mine and it wasn't a kind peace or a cruel peace, it was simply peace. How obvious I am but death is obvious, it does all the things everybody says it does. The world is wise, Maribel, learn to forgive it everything and you will find you have forgiven yourself, that's what he often said.

I kissed his forehead and backed out of the room bumping into the doorpost. He would have liked that, too. I expect he turned for a moment away from St Peter just to watch. At least I hope so. I'm certain he would hesitate at the gate of Heaven wondering if the place might not lack a certain grist for his pen.

I thanked his wife or whoever she was. She nodded and said a number of other guests were below waiting to pay their last respects. I went quickly down the stairs and into the courtyard where there was now a knot of people, all men, all importantly dressed, all talking in low, confident voices. I hurried past them out into the street. The sun was shining.

I walked back to the square. It seemed a long way, I think I got lost because I kept looking at the people, I couldn't stop myself. I was in a foolish state of mind or was I? It was as if my mind was smiling, as if inside my head there was sunshine, too. And some smiled back and one or two even said good day to me as though I was like them and they knew it, could recognise me as one of themselves and I didn't object, nothing in me objected, nothing at all. There was a small church, I went in down some narrow steps. It was quiet after the hubbub of the street. I dipped my hand in the holy water, crossed myself and then knelt, just there where I was. I cried then, I cried but it wasn't from a broken heart but a whole heart overflowing with something I couldn't understand and my head was saying it doesn't matter if you don't know what is happening to you, don't try to understand, simply accept, accept. Accept what? What? No answer came and yet I was comforted.

In the square I behaved more soberly. I bought a glass

125

of sharp wine from a stall and I sat in the sun to drink it. Not a single beggar approached me. They know their business. I could see everything more steadily now. I could see him in that modest room, I could see him in my own, and I think, think, I think I heard him say, had he ever said it to me? I don't know, I don't think so but it was his voice saying, I speak of you not as you are, Maribel, but as I should wish you to be, which made no sense, what do you mean, what do you mean? I was asking aloud and there was a fat man in black velvet looking puzzled and saying, I said, are you free, young woman, are you free? And I jumped up, laughing, and said, yes, yes, yes! He didn't understand, of course, when I walked away. He became persistent, abusive. I told him he had misunderstood me, an understandable, natural mistake, but I was not as it happened for hire.

I can't pay for these lodgings after tomorrow. I shall have to move. I don't know what I shall do, there are holes in my stockings, my shoes need mending, I haven't eaten all day but I shall go down into the square again soon. And if anyone asks me, I don't suppose they will and I shall never volunteer the information, if anyone does ask my opinion of Miguel de Cervantes I shall say that when I knew him he was human to a fault.

From my hand 23rd April 1616, Madrid.[1]

[1] This last entry would appear to confirm that Cervantes died on Friday 22nd April 1616 as Astrana Marín has argued and not on Saturday 23rd April, the traditional date. María Isabel writing on Saturday says she saw him the day before.

✺ EPILOGUE ✺

Maria Isabel's later life is unrecorded. Two possible references to her remain but the evidence they offer is circumstantial; at best one may say they are consistent with a future which may have been hers. One relates to a trial for theft in May 1616 in Madrid and the other is a memorial tablet dated 29th June 1645 in the church of San Martín, Río, Puerto Rico.

The name which may be hers appears in a list of defendants tried in Madrid on 4th May 1616. The name María Isabel Echauri y Pradillo de Caparroso agrees with her own hysterical announcement of herself during dinner at Epiphany but the court's list does not include her title of duchess. Jerónimo was the Duke of Caparroso and Echauri y Pradillo would be her maiden name, it being the custom in Spain for a woman to keep her own name and to place her husband's after it. Possibly her title was omitted in an attempt to avoid further social disgrace or because Jerónimo had already procured an annulment of the marriage, though this seems unlikely: such processes were never easily or quickly completed in 17th-century Spain despite the interwoven corruption of church and state. Against the name is written: acquitted for the theft of a pair of shoes upon the surety of Count Enrique Braja. It is conceivable that Braja whom María Isabel had seen but not spoken to at mass in Guadalajara may have come to her rescue.

The tablet in San Martín, Río, Puerto Rico, honours the memory of the beloved wife of Don Juan José de Fuentes. The name, with de Fuentes substituted for de Caparroso, is the same. It states that María Isabel departed this sublunary scene on 29th June 1645 at the age of fifty-nine and was mourned by her husband, children and friends. This might suggest that she travelled to the West Indies to join her successful brothers and remarried there.